Don't Shoot The Harbinger

About the Author

Ryan is a long time writer who spent several years struggling to become a first time author. He is a father, a husband, and a friend. He can't think of anything else to describe himself, handsome maybe.

Disclaimer

This is a work of fiction. Names, characters, businesses, places, events, locales, and incidents are either the products of the author's imagination or used in a fictitious manner. Any resemblance to actual persons, living or dead, or actual events is purely coincidental.

Follow at: www.amazon.com/author/greenryan
https://twitter.com/xxtheryangreen

Cover design and layout by Samantha Green © 2021

Dedicated to Mom and Dad

2020 took you both from me.
Thank you for always believing in me.
It couldn't take that.

Chapter One

      Tonight is a big night for Blaine. He and Megan have been together for nearly four years and he knows that it is well past time for them to take the next step. They live together, they sleep together, they eat together, they even have a dog together, something Blaine was originally against but Megan ultimately talked him into. Blaine knows that it is time for them to settle down, get married and start having children.

Megan is more than ready, she has been hinting at it for months now. Every opportunity she gets she hints at the fact that he hasn't proposed to her yet. When he is around her family they make sure to remind him of how great Megan is and how cute their children would be.

He knows that, he has just been biding his time waiting for the perfect moment. Blaine came to the realization that Megan wasn't going to stick around forever and he had better get serious sooner than later.

Blaine has been at work since 6 AM this morning finishing up on work projects that he has been putting off getting started on all week. He knows that after tonight he won't want to have to think about anything related to work so he is trying to cram in as much as he can now.

Megan and Blaine have dinner plans tonight at 8 PM. It is currently 5 PM, Blaine promised Megan that he would be home by 4 PM so that they wouldn't feel rushed getting ready to head out to dinner.

He knows that he needs to do something to make it up to her. He stops by the florist on the way home and picks up a bouquet of flowers. It has all of the normal flowers a man would think to pick up for a woman; red and white roses, baby's breath and Blaine knows that Megan especially loves Lavender. The red and purple tend to contrast a little bit Blaine thinks as he has the florist put it together but he knows that Megan will love it anyway.

When Blaine comes into the house he hears Megan shouting from the bathroom "Babe, we don't have much time just come hop in here with me."

"You don't have to tell me twice," Blaine shouts back to her.

He brings the bouquet into the bathroom with him. Megan opens the shower curtain and she smiles at him. "You are too sweet, get in here."

Blaine gets into the shower.

Once he gets inside she begins kissing him and takes his hands and pulls him in close. She wraps his arms around her and presses them to her butt.

"I have a surprise for you too," Megan tells Blaine.

"But you hate having sex in the shower"

"I do, but we can try it again. It's our anniversary, I want to do something different for it and we're in a hurry."

They continue kissing under the warm downpour from the faucet above them and they are doing their best to avoid drowning from a lack of air and gallons of water pouring over them by switching positions under the water and moving the spray nozzle up and down.

"Blaine this thing is not working" Megan says as she points down to her crotch and they both start laughing.

"Okay I was wrong, I remember why I hate it. It just feels so dry."

They both continue laughing.

"Should we just finish this after dinner?" Blaine asks Megan.

"We can wait until then I suppose."

They get out of the shower and they walk to their bedroom and begin to dry off. Megan has laid out an outfit for Blaine on the bed.

"I think you would look very handsome in this" she tells him as she picks it up and holds it to his body.

"Is that new?" Blaine asks Megan.

"Yes, I took the liberty of going out today and picking you out a nice outfit for tonight. You have been talking about how amazing this restaurant was and I wanted us both to look the part. I thought it would be nice for us to walk in and everyone just be floored at how great we looked, now you especially."

Blaine takes it from her "I'm here to impress you and you alone." Blaine leans in and kisses Megan.
Blaine finishes drying off and he gets dressed. He walks out to the living room and puts on some music while Megan finishes getting dressed and putting on her makeup to get ready.

He sits down and he starts reading through some old running magazines until Megan appears from the bedroom.

He looks up at her and she is wearing a black dress with a slim fitting top that cuts just deep enough to let her cleavage peek through. The dress has half sleeves that go just past her elbows and she is wearing a flowing black and white chevron patterned skirt that lands just above her knees. Her legs are shining as the light hits them from the body dew she applied and she has on black matte leather flats.

"You look gorgeous" Blaine tells Megan in the most sincere complementary way a man can tell a woman that he has already seen every inch of and isn't looking for anything in return.

Megan blushes a little bit "we're going to be late."

"Blaine walks over to Megan and he grabs her by the hips "why don't we just stay in tonight and I can just watch you slip that dress on and off a couple times, that would definitely be more pleasing for me at least."

"We will have plenty of time for that after dinner." Megan says to Blaine.

"Yeah but we still have some time."

Megan slowly turns around and she grabs Blaine by his belt buckle and she guides him to the bedroom. They walk through the hallway to the bedroom and Megan pulls him and positions him in front of their bed. She starts to unbuckle Blaine's belt

and she unbuttons his pants. She pulls the dress shirt out from his pants and she begins to unbutton it from the bottom button up to the neck. Blaine begins to kiss her on her lips and she pulls away.

She puts a finger to her lips and she waves it side to side signaling to him that she wants to experiment on the side of fun rather than the traditional intimacy tonight. She continues to undress Blaine removing his shirt back and discarding it on the floor and she pulls his undershirt off over his head. Next on her list are the rest of the pants and she drops to her knees as she slowly slides them down. As they make their way just below Blaine's waist his hard penis suddenly and quickly springs upward towards Megan's face behind the thin fabric of Blaine's underwear.

She grabs onto it and she presses her lips to it as she slowly starts sliding her hand back and forth on his shaft on the outside of his underwear as Blaine begins to close his eyes and shift and nudge back and forth. For Blaine the first minute of his erection is when it is the most sensitive and pleasurable and he is making sure to enjoy it while it lasts.

Megan stops, she knows this as well.

She removes Blaine's underwear and she pushes him onto the bed. Blaine scoots himself to the head of the bed and sits up to see Megan.

She begins to take off her dress slowly for him, she reaches back and slides the zipper down and the dress falls to her feet. She turns around so her back is facing Blaine and she starts to shake her hips back and forth as she unbuttons her shirt. She bends down and she slowly takes off her flats making sure that Blaine can see just enough of her body peeking around the slim piece of thong fabric that is resting between her butt cheeks.

She stands back up, and completely removes her top and she reaches behind her back and undoes her bra. She pulls her bra down and her breasts become completely exposed. She starts to pinch her nipples a little bit to start making them erect.

"You know I hate how my nipples look when they're soft" Megan says to Blaine lying in front of him and Blaine smiles softly at her.

She walks to Blaine and climbs up onto the bed and she is on her hands and knees. She crawls up to Blaine and she continues taking off his underwear. She positions her body perpendicular to Blaine's with her upper body hovering over Blaine's midsection while facing toward him. She grabs Blaine's hand as she opens her legs and she guides his ring and middle fingers inside of her. The second the fingers cross the cusp of the inside of her vagina she closes her eyes and she takes a deep breath in, she smiles and lets out a small moan.

"Just like that, slow," Megan says to Blaine.

Megan looks at Blaine and asks him "Do you remember the day we met?"

"Of course I do. Why do you ask?"

"I want to hear it from your perspective. I know how I remember it. How do you remember it?"

"Right now?" Blaine asks Megan.

"From my perspective there would be no better time to hear it than now"

"But we're naked and we have to get to dinner soon."

"We are about to share the most passionate and intense orgasm of our shared lives and I would love to hear about the way you felt on the day we met as we lay here intertwined in each other's naked bodies. Dinner can wait, we can be a little late."

Chapter Two

It was a Sunday morning and I was sitting at a coffee shop near my work. I had just finished a project at work that I had been racking my brains over for the last two months. I hadn't taken a day off from this work since I started and I had been working through the night most nights.

After work I changed into my running clothes and I ran my daily three miles that I had been holding myself to for a few years now at that point. It was around 60 degrees so the run didn't make me too sweaty and smelly so I thought I would stop into the coffee shop and not be too offensive to anyone near me.

The barista behind the counter was a blonde haired busty woman wearing an olive green long sleeve shirt. She was cute enough from what I remember but she had nothing on you.

Megan smiles at Blaine, "such a sweet talker."

I remember that a woman was sitting a few tables away from me. She was wearing a purple shirt if I remember correctly. I had seen her talking to the barista on and off since she got there. This wasn't the first time that I had seen this woman.

I remember that she began talking to herself as if she was having a full on conversation with another person. It was super weird that's why I can remember everything about that so vividly. Suddenly the woman stopped talking and she acted as if the person she was talking to got up and she was now watching someone walk to the bathroom.

I stood up from the table and I walked over to the woman and introduced myself to her.

"Hello I'm Blaine, I see you come here all the time and I just wanted to introduce myself" I said to her.

"My name is Alex."

"Is that short for anything?" I asked her.

"Alexandria."

"It's nice to meet you Alex."

"Blaine? That was your name?"

"Yes."

"I'm sorry Blaine I don't want to waste your time. I'm in a relationship. My girlfriend Aimee just went to the bathroom, I'm sure you're just being nice and you weren't aware that she was my girlfriend but she will be coming back any moment and I really don't want to explain myself to her."

I walked back to my table and I sat down. I stared into my cup of nitro cold brew with a shot of butterscotch the same thing I always ordered.

"You still always order that" Megan chimes in.

I had lived in this new city for almost a year now at that point and I hadn't had a single date, not a single meaningful conversation, not a wink, not a nod, nothing but maybe that's what I needed after everything I just escaped from. It was then that I quickly and carelessly stood up from my table without giving a thought to whether someone may be walking by and I bumped into a young woman who was in fact walking by.

She spilled her drink all over herself and I immediately began to apologize to her.

"I am so so sorry" I said as I reached for a pile of napkins and handed them to her. "I am so stupid I can't believe I did that. Please let me buy you a new drink" I offered her as some kind of shitty and meaningless consultation for the consequences of me completely ruining her clothes.

The woman looked up from patting her shirt dry and she made eye contact with me. I can still remember the look on her face. She was a lot less pissed off at me than she had every single right to be.

"I would love that," she told me.

I was speechless, I continued staring at the woman trying to find the words to respond, at that point literally any words would do. But all I could find from within my stupid and nervous self was a sound that resembled a mix of a deep guttural gulp and a loud exclaiming yelp.

The woman blushed and she reached her hand out to me.

"Hi, I'm Megan," she said, introducing herself to me.

"I am Blaine " I responded introducing myself to her.

You grabbed me by the hand and you led me to a table in the corner of the coffee shop. You sat down against the window

and you motioned for me to take a seat directly across from you.

I sat down.

I reached into my pocket and I pulled out a twenty dollar bill and punched my arm out toward you. I had forgotten how to control all of my fine motor skills and my ability to speak in any recognizable manner had gone out the window.

"I'll be right back" you said as you got up and walked away from the table. I thought you were probably going to just keep going and never come back after you saw how helpless I was.

I remember I just stared at you as you walked to the counter and then something miraculous happened. You started to come back, and I couldn't take my eyes off of you.

You came back to the table and you set your drink down.

I looked up at you and behind you was a plate glass window, displaying dozens of skyscrapers standing hundreds of feet tall extending into the clouds.

I had walked that street hundreds of times. At all times of the day, from dusk until dawn, from sunrise to sunset, I dissected those buildings from the ground to the sky. I had been towered over by those magnificent feats of architecture on numerous occasions.

But it wasn't until this moment, there with you that I had ever felt so small. I had never felt the presence of another object, let alone another being dwarfing me like that.

I knew that I felt that way for a reason.

Something about you on that day was special, not just special, you were distinguished, destined to be significant in some way to my life and I could sense it.

"Blaine. Do you want to get out of here and go for a walk? I'd like to get to know you better, but I really need to change my clothes and I don't live far from here" you asked me.

"Sure."

I stood up and you grabbed my hand and guided me out of the coffee shop.

"My apartment is just a few blocks north of here, do you want to come back with me while I change? Then maybe we can go get breakfast somewhere" you asked.

"Sure."

"Are the only words you're going to be able to get out of your body for the rest of the day 'sure' and that weird groaning gurgle?" you questioned me playfully.

"No."

"And no as well?" you added to your extensive list of cross examination questions.

"I can talk, I just, I don't know if it's just that this whole interaction has really caught me off guard. I was sitting in a coffee shop, full of women, none of which would ever have an interest in me then literally, quite literally our worlds collide" I tried to explain to you.

"Blaine, that is how most organic friendships occur. Not everyone can meet on the computer or through a message board. Most people just run into each other somewhere they both frequent at an opportune time. Don't think too much into it, what's more strange is how often I go there and I never see you" you said to me.

"I'm usually at work at this time of the morning."

"Ahh and you weren't today?" your inquiry continued.

"No, today I finished a big project I had been working on to kind of celebrate, well, not so much to celebrate but to commemorate the fact I decided to treat myself."

"See, what I mean? It is more strange from my perspective that you would be there today. I am there every Sunday at this time. You are never there, I'm the one who should be taken back by our meeting. You just broke your routine for one day and ruined a lady's new wardrobe."

This conversation played as the soundtrack for the quick few block walk back to your apartment because before either of us really could grasp the magnitude of this seemingly chance encounter we were at the doorstep of your apartment.

"The choice is yours Blaine. Do you want to stay out here while I go up and change my clothes or do you want to come up there and risk seeing the inside of my apartment and becoming even more dazed and inarticulate?" you honestly asked of me.

Megan interjects herself into the story.

"I really wanted you to come up. For numerous reasons, the most obvious one being that I wanted to see you pass out when I 'accidentally' let you see me in my underwear" Megan put finger air quotes up for the word accidentally.

"Very funny," Blaine says to Megan.

"Soooo you want to come up then?" you asked me.

"Sure" I responded back to you resorting to my nervous fight or flight predetermined set of responses.

"You promised you would say more than sure."

You smiled at me and grabbed my hand again and led me inside. You lived on the ground floor about five doors in.

"Wow that's awfully close to the street, that must be great when you have to bring in groceries, do you pay extra for that?" I asked you.

"I usually have my groceries delivered to me and no it's actually cheaper. Instead of one upstairs neighbor dancing and having sex in their kitchen at 3 a.m. every night I have twenty more floors of neighbors above me doing it. All of that concentrated sound just builds up and by the time it gets to me it's like a huge sonic boom of moans and groans and grunts and thumps" you explained to me.

"I'm sorry I asked."

You opened the door to your apartment and welcomed me in with a shoeing gesture.

"See for yourself."

I walked in and I looked around trying to analyze as much about you as humanly possible within a 5 second span. I didn't want to come across as too interested where I was just nervously looking at every little thing in your apartment.

I walked over to your couch and I sat down.

"Is this a good place for me to sit?" I asked.

"That's a weird question, I don't think anyone has ever asked me before while they were sitting on my couch."

You walked down a hallway and into a room at the end of the hallway.

The spot I chose to sit had a perfect line of sight into your bedroom, this was not at all intentional.

I see you reappear in the doorway and you are just in your bra and panties. You shut the door to your bedroom. You shouted out from behind the door "Did you pick that spot because you knew you would be able to see into my bedroom, pervert?"

I bolted up from the couch and walked to the end of the hallway and nervously began trying to explain myself to you.

"No, no I swear that I had no idea. I promise, I wouldn't try to do that. I just picked a seat honestly, I asked you if it was okay" I tried explaining myself to you honestly.

You re-emerged from behind that closed door. You were wearing a loose gray cardigan over top of a long sleeve red shirt and black leggings.

21

"Calm down, I was just kidding. How could you possibly know where my bedroom was going to be? Besides, what makes you think that by not warning you I didn't want you to see that?" she flirtatiously said to me in a way I can only assume was meant to completely break me down into a nervous wreck.

"Well, did you?" I asked you.

"Did I what?" You asked as you smiled at me. "Did you think about where you wanted to eat yet?"

"Well we've already had coffee and I'm not really in the mood for breakfast food, what do you suggest around here?" I asked you.

"I know of a little deli that has awesome bagels. You can get them with like fifty different kinds of cream cheeses or whatever you want on them"

"Sounds great to me"

We walked a few blocks east of your apartment and we both used the time to try and find out as much about the other as possible, or as much as we were willing to tell the other.

"Where did you grow up Blaine?" you asked me.

I had never really had an in depth conversation about my past with someone I just met. I didn't know what I could and couldn't tell you or what I should and should not confess. I decided to play it as carefully as possible, after all they just met.

"I am from the Midwest, and you?"

"I am from here. My family has been in this area for generations, they moved out here during the gold rush as far as I know and they made themselves comfortable."

There was a homeless man standing outside of the deli asking for change and I was a little nervous about the guy but your body language told me that the man was harmless.

"HI MEGAN!" the man shouted as he walked towards you.

"MY EYE IS DOING MUCH BETTER!" he pointed to his eye as he yelled at you.

"That's great to hear. My friend Blaine has never been here before, what would you suggest to him?"

The man walked over to me and put his hand on my shoulder. "You have to get the salmon cream cheese on a jalapeno bagel, I eat two everyday to help keep me strong."

"Well if that's what you suggest, I guess I'll take your word for it."

You grabbed my hand and we walked into the deli.

"So what's the deal with that guy?" I asked you.

"He's harmless. He doesn't really have anywhere to go so he spends most of his time out front there. Whenever I come through here I buy him something."

"I'm really not a fan of salmon, do you think he would care if I didn't order it? I mean, he seems kind of out there, he won't like to try and kill me for not getting what he suggested will he?"

I nervously stared at you waiting for you to reassure me that I would be safe.

"Oh, you're serious? No. No he will not kill you for ordering a different kind of cream cheese than what he likes. You are something else, Blaine."

"Would you mind if we just went somewhere else? I really don't feel comfortable here right now"

"Well, if I were you I would at least order a bagel to go and give it to him on your way out. If you're not going to eat at his favorite deli you gotta sweeten him up somehow, otherwise he may actually kill you."

I was unsure if you were joking with me and I nervously chuckled at your statement.

"Dear god Blaine, just order something. I promise you this place is very good and he will not hurt you. He is harmless."

"Fine, I will give it a try"

I spent a few minutes looking at the menu board. You were not lying, they must have had fifty different kinds of spreads for the bagels and probably an equal amount of varieties of bagels themselves. There was a selection of sliced meats and cheeses you could add to the bagels as well.

"It might be a little early for corned beef or pastrami on a Sunday," Blaine jokes to Megan.

"I was thinking the same thing, it does sound good though.

I nod in agreement.

The young girl behind the counter is starting to get restless "Are you ready to order?" she asks.

"Oh I'm sorry" I explained. "There is just so much to think about."

You stepped forward to the counter.

"I will have a cinnamon and raisin bagel with cranberry cream cheese spread. Also one jalapeno bagel with the salmon spread."

The girl behind the counter looked at me "And for you?" she asked.

"Roasted red pepper and cucumber spread on an onion poppy seed bagel"

You looked at me and said, "I don't think I have ever seen anyone order that combination."

"I know I got nervous, that girl is intimidating."

The girl grabbed the three bagels from behind the counter and put them in the toaster. "Would you like anything to drink with these?"

"Two red bulls," you said.

"One of those sugar free" I chimed in.

The girl grabbed the drinks from the cooler and set them on the counter. The timer for the bagels went off and she grabbed them from the toaster. She put the spread on the three bagels and put them in their individual bags and set them on the counter.

She began ringing up the order on her cash register "$16.40."

You reached into your purse and began digging around.

"No, let me get this, it's the least I could do for ruining your shirt earlier." Blaine reaches into his pocket and pulls out his wallet. He removes a twenty dollar bill and hands it to the girl behind the counter.

The girl rings us in and hands me my change. I took the food from the lady and threw the leftover change into her tip jar.

"We can give these few dollars to your friend outside" I told you.

You smiled at me "Sounds like a plan."

We head out of the deli and Blaine hands the bagel and the handful of singles to the man standing outside.

"Wow Blaine, thank you so much. No wonder Megan loves you so much, you are very nice."

You started laughing "I love him now? Why do you say that?"

"Well you brought him to meet your best friend and to your favorite place to eat that's what I do when I love someone"

You were laughing still and said "Good point. You have a great day John."

John grabbed me and hugged me really tight, I was really uncomfortable but I didn't want you to see "Thanks John, I appreciate it."

You begin walking and I break away from the hug and walk quickly to catch up with you.

"Where do we go from here?" I ask.

Blaine and Megan pull into the parking lot of the restaurant, Blaine pulls into a parking spot, unbuckles his seatbelt and turns the car off.

"Where are you going? You aren't done with the story yet?" Megan asks him.

"We have a reservation Megan." Blaine explains.

"It will be fine, you're just now getting to the good parts."

Chapter Three

I was aimlessly following you as you weaved in and out of
alleyways and jaywalking through crosswalks until you
finally stopped.

"Were here" you exclaimed.

I looked around at my surroundings "This park? We
walked by at least five parks on our way here."

"I know but those parks weren't this park"

"What is so special about this park?"

"You'll see, just be patient."

"We walked by that one park with all of the green houses
and the flower gardens. It had that little lake thing and a
fountain thing."

"That's Wright park and if you really want to go back to it
we can, but I promise you that you will love where I am
taking you. Trust me Blaine there are like five parks around
this area and none of them have a thing on this one."

You stood behind Me and put your hands over my eyes
"just keep walking."

You guide me towards the water, I can feel the breeze
coming off of the Puget Sound on my face "Now open your
eyes" you tell me.

I opened my eyes and there was a giant globe in front of me with the backdrop of the ocean behind it.

"That's really cool, I'm not sure if it's as cool as the other park though, that one had a waterpark in it."

"Look around you Blaine."

The globe was sitting atop a stone paved compass with a crescent moon stained into the cement just beyond it.

"Look at the water Blaine."

I looked at the water and there were several ships and boats that were docked and then off in the distance I saw something. I squinted for a few seconds to help me see and suddenly it became perfectly clear.

"That globe overlooking the mountain is the best thing in this entire city" You tell me.

"Mount Rainier" I chimed in.

"If you want to fit in around here Blaine just call it the mountain"

"If you can come to this spot and take in this view and not feel anything, you are not a human being capable of feeling anything. At any moment that volcanic mountain could erupt and all of this would just be gone. The earth, the moon, the stars, the water, all of it. It would all be covered in ash and fire yet here we stand. We doubt its power, we live at its feet out of ignorance and foolishness." You explain to me.

"That was really dark Megan, if that's what comes to mind when you come here I can't make sense of why you would like to come here. It just reminds you that at any point in time you could be dead"

"You are absolutely right, But am I dead? Whatever it is that chooses when we are born and when we die has decided to spare my life, to spare the lives of everyone in this city. You have to appreciate that. Whether it be god, or fate or just chance, you have to appreciate the overall magnitude and the irony of this globe and this moon in front of the sound. This area has been destroyed before and it will be destroyed again, but we are here today, living, breathing and talking about it."

You turn to me and you grab my face and you kiss me on the lips.

"And now we are kissing here Blaine. Alright, now you tell me exactly what you have seen in this city and I want to fill in the gaps for you."

"Honestly Megan, I really haven't seen anything. When I moved here I made the choice to just hide away and work and stay under the radar. I left a lot of stuff back home and I just wanted a simple life here."

"Well then we have a lot we need to see by the end of the day."

31

"This next one is going to be your choice. I'm going to give you three options and I want you to pick one. Now remember we can always go back and look at the other two some other day. I just don't want to overload your brain with new sights in such a short amount of time. Plus I'm not sure if I can top where your childhood love had prom." You asked me.

"Got it."

"Would you rather see the TAM, the Washington State History Museum or The Museum of Glass?"

"What the hell is a TAM?" I remember saying to you because you for whatever reason expected me to know what it was.

Well you lived in the city for like a year at the time Blaine.

"The Tacoma Art Museum."

"Ohhhhh. Well damn that's a hard choice. I've been to several art museums and history museums, which one do you think is better? I mean I really like both things a lot."

"Well if it helps you make your choice a little easier, the Museum of Glass also has something called a Bridge of Glass leading up to it."

"Museum of Glass! I picked the Museum of Glass."

"Great, there's also a really cute coffee shop right in front of the entrance to the bridge we can stop at. But before you get yourself too worked up, the bridge itself isn't made of glass, it just has like a bunch of glass sculptures and exhibits on it too. Actually, what day is it Blaine!?!""

"June 18th why?"

"I don't know how I forgot! The Taste of Tacoma festival is today, that's why everything has been so empty! It's going on right now we should go. It's right by the zoo as well if you want to see that too."

"Yeah, I've seen a bunch of fliers for that everywhere that we've gone today but I didn't know what it was. Taste of Tacoma? Is there like a ton of crowds and stuff?"

"Well yeah it's like the biggest event the city has other than the fireworks on the 4th of July. But it will be fun I promise. There's like 100 different food vendors and drinks and a carnival. There's music and games and there is so much stuff to do."

"Fine, I'll go. But if we run into any of your ex boyfriends or a group of your friends you're not going to bail on me or something are you?"

"I might, I can't promise that." You tell me with a straight face so that I can't tell if you're joking.

I stare at you until you start to smile a little bit.

"No, I wouldn't do that to you."

"Can we see the zoo first? Honestly, it's been the one thing I've really wanted to see in this city since I moved here."

"Then why haven't you gone yet?"

"I didn't want to just go alone."

"You are something else Blaine, I go and do stuff on my own all the time."

"Well you are a lot more comfortable by yourself in this city than me I guess."

"The zoo is a few miles away. Do you want to get an Uber or something?" You ask me.

"Sure. But I don't have the app on my phone, do you?"

"How do you get around the city if you don't use Uber?"

"The bus mostly I guess, or I just use my bike."

"You must waste a lot of time because it takes forever to get anywhere on the bus. I'll get the uber, don't worry."

The uber arrived and pulled up on the street next to us.

The driver got out of his Silver Honda SUV, "Hello are you Morgan?" he asked us.

"Umm, my name is Megan." you snarkily responded to him.

"The Uber driver checks his phone again. "I'm so sorry, yes, it says Megan." He opened the driver side rear door for Megan. "Are you coming too Blaine?"

I started to walk around the back side of the SUV. "Wait, how did you know my name?" I asked the driver.

"Your girlfriend just said it out loud buddy" he says to me.

"Oh yeah, that makes sense I guess." I walked around the back side of the SUV and got into the back next to you.

The short car ride there you and the driver were having an awkward small talk conversation about the Taste of Tacoma festival. The driver was upset that he couldn't make it but the money had been great all day for traffic to the event.

"We're actually going to the zoo first then heading over to the event." you tell the driver.

"Ahh well you both have fun today. Don't drink too much and be safe."

We pull up in front of the zoo at the designated drop off area and we both get out and meet on the curb.

The driver rolls his passenger window down and says "Be sure to rate me 5 starts please" then speeds off.

"What did the app say his name was?" I ask you.

"Umm hold on." You pulled your phone out of your purse "It says his name is Shawn, how come?"

"He knew my name. I know for a fact you never said my name out loud while he was around. How would he know my name?"

"Maybe I accidentally listed your name on the pickup details or something, I'm not sure. Did he look familiar to you? Have you ever seen him anywhere else?"

"No, no nothing like that. It was just strange that he knew my name."

"Well, let's not let that ruin our day Blaine. We're here! The zoo! Let's go in!"

We go into the zoo and you grab a map off of a kiosk sitting just beyond the entrance. You look at it for a few minutes before deciding the path to take to see everything we can in as little time as possible.

"Since we're kind of in a little bit of a rush, follow me, I'll make sure we see all of the best animals and exhibits so we have a good amount of time for the festival."

"That's fine."

"What do you mean? What's wrong, Blaine. Are you still mad about that Uber driver?"

"No, just, don't worry about it. Let's have fun, I don't want to rush through here and not really get to experience everything here with you."

"Blaine, we could just sit in a park bench the rest of the day not really doing anything and I would be happy as long as I was able to do it with you"

I look over at you and I gaze into your eyes and I can't believe you are returning these feelings that I am feeling so strongly for you. I had never felt like this about a woman and I know that no one had ever felt this toward me.

You grab my hand.

"Blaine, can I ask you something?"

"Yeah sure."

You walk to a park bench a few feet away and we both sit down.

"Do you see that girl over there?" You point to a girl standing nearby drinking from a water fountain.

"Yes, why?"

"Do you like what she is wearing?" you ask me.

I scan the girl up and down.

"It's fine I guess. It's just a normal top and some leggings."

"How do you feel about that weird pattern she has on her mumble pants? Do you think it's supposed to be ironic that she wore leopard print to the zoo? Or do you think she did it on purpose?" you asked me.

"Wait, what the hell are mumble pants?"

"Mumble pants, you've never heard them called that?"

"Absolutely not. Why the hell would they be called that?"

"All kinds of girls refer to them as mumble pants Blaine. You really need to get out more."

"Well that doesn't really help. Why do you or they or all of you call them 'mumble pants'?" Blaine asks with the most sincere level of ignorance and intrigue.

"There she's facing us. Now look closely. See if you can figure it out."

"Does it have anything to do with the pattern on them because it's an animal print?"

"No they could be solid black, it wouldn't matter."

"Umm is it like a lazy pants kind of thing? Like they could be pajamas or something but girls wear them formally or just instead of pants?"

"That makes no sense, you're just saying anything at this point."

"I have no idea Megan. I don't even want to guess anymore, I just sound dumb."

"Look really closely at her crotch, Blaine. Do you notice anything?"

"Umm do you mean like a camel toe or something?"

"You're getting warmer."

"I really have no idea what camel toe and mumbling has to do with each other." I exclaimed loudly.

The girl in the cheetah print leggings looked intently at us and walked away.

"It's really pretty simple. Mumble pants, you can see her lips moving, but you can't make out what they're saying.."

I stared at you until you stood up and you grabbed me by the hand and pulled me up from the bench.

"The Asian Forest Sanctuary exhibit is this way Blaine. Do you want to look at the map so you can get an idea of what animals are in each exhibit?"

"No, it's okay, I trust you'll give me a good tour."

You smiled at me "The Asian Forest Sanctuary is probably my second favorite part of this zoo. It has a tiger, it has a leopard and it's where the elephants are. I think this is probably the part of the zoo that gets the busiest because not a lot of places have tigers and leopards."

"You sure are one well educated tour guide for a zoo that you don't work out."

"I've been coming here ever since I was little so I know this place inside and out.

You and I enter the exhibit area and the first animal exhibit we come across is the Elephants. There are large mounds of dirt, big rocks and large puddles of standing water everywhere. The elephants are behind a wire fence a few feet away from where the crowds can stand.

"You'd think it would smell a lot worse around this area considering the amount of elephants and the size of their dumps" Blaine blurts out loud and everyone around them looks at him.

"Yeah they do a pretty good job of keeping all of the areas fairly clean."

We are standing in front of the exhibit when an elephant walks over to a pool of water. The elephant scoops up a large amount of water in its trunk and sprays it at me.

"It must have heard you , Blaine." you said as you are laughing at me.

"Can we see the next animal?"

We came across the Clouded Leopard exhibit. There is a large netted area behind glass covered on tree branches and foliage.

"I don't see anything" I tell you.

"I'm not sure. Last time I was here there was a Mother and a few babies. Maybe the weather isn't right? I'm not sure what kind of weather they prefer but it is kind of warm. They're probably in their little cave area keeping cool."

"That sucks, I hope the Tigers aren't doing the same."

We walk to the Tiger exhibit and there is a large grass fielded area with a ledge overlooking a large man made pond. The tigers are playing with each other on the ledge jumping up and down and splashing through the water.

"Now this is what I wanted to see!" I yelled "Finally some animals are playing with each other!"

"You are really excited about this zoo huh?" you asked me.

"Yeah. I guess animals are just the one thing I've always been able to relate to. I never had a lot of friends growing

41

up like I mentioned earlier so I would go to zoos and aquariums a lot for fun."

"That is sort of sad, and it's sort of lame" you said to me as you kiss me on the cheek to make sure that I know you're being playful.

"Next up is the Penguins Blaine!" you yelled at me.

"They're all kind of socially awkward like you, walking around and throwing rocks at each other and pushing each other over and what not."

"I have always sort of related to penguins so I guess that makes sense." I explain to you.

"I really can see it, they are easy to relate to. Do you know what my favorite thing about penguins is Blaine?"

"That they are monogamous? That they pick a partner and they will mate for life with them? That they will give their partner a rock to symbolize their love and they pair off for eternity?"

"Well, no, I read that was actually not true."

"I was going to say that to you once you said 'yeah'."

"My favorite part about penguins is when they slide on their stomachs across ice and stuff, that is hilarious." you tell me.

"Blaine there are still a few more exhibits here but because we saw your favorite animals do you mind if we jump ahead and see mine? We can always come back on another day and really take our time. I just"

I cut you off.

"Absolutely. I'm glad that you were willing to compromise and let me see this much of the zoo. What is your favorite part?"

"Follow me."

You begin to lead me into an area called "The Red Wolf Woods."

As soon as we enter the exhibit you run up to the glass "Look there is a litter of puppies! Blaine come look!"

I run to the glass not trailing far behind you.

"Oh Wow! I had no idea that there was a Wolf exhibit here!"

"They're not just any wolves, they're Red Wolves. They are critically endangered and we are lucky enough to be looking at some of the very last ones in the world. These puppies are so important, they could literally be the last hope to bring back their species from the brink of extinction"

"If there is one thing I have learned about you today Megan it's that you really have a penchant for favoring things with a really bleak and daunting future."

"How do you mean?"

"The point is the sound you liked because the volcano could kill everyone, the wolves you like because they are almost all extinct. You just really seem to like things that hint towards disaster."

"That is a really shitty and pessimistic way to look at it. Maybe I like those things because it makes me realize how special and fragile life is. Maybe I like those things because it makes me think about how lucky I am to be able to wake up in the morning and go to a coffee house and meet a new friend and tour the city and go to the zoo. Maybe I am just happy to be alive and enjoy every second of my life without having to overanalyze it and examine it under some microscope of shit where I just think everything and everyone is horrible."

"No, no that's not what I mean, I'm sorry."

"I can't believe you are going to try and ruin the wolves for me. I didn't ruin the penguins for you. I didn't complain about how much the exhibit smelled like penguin shit. I didn't talk about how all of the penguins in the world are going to be dead soon because of global warming and the only ones we'll be able to look at are in stupid zoos around the world. I didn't make fun of you because they are stupid animals who just waddle around and drown and they are like the only bird who can't swim because they're so dumb and fat."

"No. You did not say anything like that. I'm sorry I brought it up. Can we please just go to the food fair thing now? I'm just sort of over the zoo at this point?"

"Just give me a few minutes to sit here with the wolves in silence and we can go."

I found a bench a few feet away from you and the exhibit and I sat back and watched you as you looked at the wolves.

I noticed the expressions on your face, happy, smiling, sad, frowning, laughing, you seemed to experience every emotion possible watching the wolf pups play with each other. Their Mother comes to check in on the pups and they all begin playing with her and she starts to chase them all around and your face lit up.

You turned around and you looked at me and asked "what is bleak about that? That looks like the most fun in the world. They have no idea they are the last of their kind and they are just so carefree and fun and loving. We need to live our lives more like that."

You walked toward me and then right past me and out of the exhibit.

"We can go now" you said as you passed right by me.

Chapter Four

We were walking a few feet apart for several minutes through the zoo and out of the exit until we got to the entrance of Taste of Tacoma.

"Can we please just pretend that I didn't criticize you like that?" I asked you.

"No. It was important that you told me that has been your impression of me so far. First impressions are very important."

"I don't think that's my first impression of you, that is just me being negative and me interpreting things about you in a negative way."

"Well my first impression of you is that you are scared. You are scared, you are lonely, you are unsure of yourself and you are unwelcoming. Yet, I ignored all of that and I set out to give you the best day of your life and show you around the city. I wanted to relate to you, open up to you and show you who I am. I can't help it if you don't like what I have shown you of myself."

"It's nothing like that Megan. I like you, I absolutely do, I was just trying to be funny or something, I don't know what I was doing. I just, I am not good at this kind of interaction. Can I tell you a story?"

"Sure, go ahead," Megan says to Blaine.

"My parents bought me my first personal computer when I was ten years old, up to that point my family shared a computer in the den that had a really old and shitty dial up internet and was extremely slow. I could really only play games like solitaire and use the word processor but that didn't curb my interest and

enthusiasm.

Because of the fact that I had always displayed an interest in electronics and video games, my parents decided they would buy me a personal computer for my bedroom. They even went as far as to get me my own dedicated DSL line for it.
I don't know if you remember all the specifics of everything then but that was a big deal and those things weren't exactly cheap back in the early two thousands.

When I finally received my first computer I couldn't wait to take it apart and see how it worked. I couldn't wait to browse the internet and learn all about advanced coding, HTML and JavaScript.

I didn't have a lot of friends as a child but it was easy for me to make friends on the internet. I could login to a chatroom and talk about some of my interests and within minutes there would be dozens of people wanting to talk to me.

People from all over the world were now able to communicate and come together to share stories and experiences. A 12 year old boy from the Midwest could cuddle up with a 12 year old girl in Japan in a private chat window and talk about their favorite books, anime or their countries weirdest cuisine. A 30 year old female divorcee could find a comparable man that lived near her and spark up a new romance, without fear of persecution from family and friends for dating so soon.

Any segment of society could find a support group or chat room where like minded people would gather and talk to each other. They could save each other's lives, they could let each other know that there were other people out there just like them. Their feelings of solitude, segregation and ostracizing were fleeting and eventually they would be accepted.

The internet was amazing, it was unbelievable, it was almost unfathomable at times. It truly was life changing, and it was anything that you wanted it to be.

But that openness and availability of the internet also made young and naive kids susceptible to the dangers of the ulterior motives of preying adults. As with anything good in life there is a small number of individuals who use it to take advantage of others.

Today, I don't exactly have that same passion and enthusiasm towards technology as I used to.

Relying on the internet growing up to meet friends really skewed the way that I learned to talk to people. I just get uncomfortable sometimes and I start to I don't know, sort of just resort back to being a kid almost."

Right when I started to spill my heart out to you, you blurted out loud "Visit the world food tour, it must be new this year, let's try it out."

"Is that it?" I asked you.

"Yep, that is enough of that subject, let's try some world wide cuisine. Let's get drunk and full and let's see where the rest of the night takes us, Blaine."

I was completely unsure how I should approach the rest of the day with you but it seemed like you were over our previous conflict so I decided to try and move past it.

"First stop, Ireland." you tell me.

The food that Ireland had on display was an Irish cheddar and stout dip with Irish soda bread. We place our order and add a pint of Guinness. "Slainte" you say to the man behind the table as we get our food and start walking away, eating on the move.

"Tell me about your family Megan, I've told you a little bit about mine today. I want to know more about yours. Would you be comfortable with that?" I ask you.

"Well like I said, they have always been here. My Father and my Mother grew up here. I have a brother"

Blaine cuts in on her story "What does he do? Is he older or younger?"

"He is younger, he is still in High School. He does well in school, he is autistic, well technically or more specifically he has Asperger Syndrome."

"What is the difference?" Blaine asks her with genuine curiosity but trying not to sound like an uneducated Neanderthal.

"Well from my understanding there are three forms of autism, the classic autism then there is Asperger's Syndrome and something called Pervasive Developmental Disorder."

"And he has Asperger's?" I asked.

"Yes. Of the three I've been told, well and observed first hand through him that it can often be the least challenging to overcome, thankfully. He is highly functioning, I mean I hate using that term because it makes it seem like he is broken compared to everyone else, which he is not, that's just the classification system they chose for whatever reason."

"So he is just like everyone else? Like socially and physically?"

"Oh yeah. I mean you can definitely tell in social situations he can have a little trouble picking up on social cues and he can get overwhelmed by a lot going on but other than that, it's really a non issue most of the time for him and our family."

"That isn't bad, or doesn't sound bad anyway. Do you think it's strange that autism has just recently become so prevalent? I think that's weird, it has to be something in our food or the air or something that wasn't there fifty years ago."

"I think it has always been there. I think for hundreds or thousands of years the human mind has excelled by being able to perform at a level of consciousness and understanding that is always just right above animals. We were able to develop skills that could easily be repeated and you could survive comfortably. You learned to farm or you learned to cut down trees, or some other fairly repetitive task, there were probably people called village idiots or other people that socially were considered to be mildly quirky that just didn't stand out as much because everything wasn't so in their face like it is now." you explain to me.

"How do you mean?" I asked you.

"Lets go to England and we can keep going with this conversation" you suggested to me.

The menu in England was Fish and Chips and Newcastle Ale. We ordered one of each "Cheers Then" you say to the man

behind the counter as you tilt your Newcastle toward him and we go sit down at a nearby table and split it.

51

You continued explaining to me your take on modern autism diagnoses in the world.

"Over the last lets say seventy years technology has completely exploded. We went from black and white TV and four channels to having the internet in our pockets basically overnight."

"Well seventy years is sort of a long time."

"In terms of a single human life, yes. In terms of the course of the evolution of the human brain, not at all. If we just went back to the beginning of the modern timeline of BC and AD then human existence is roughly 2000 years old. We know that is not true because we have proof of humans existing long before that. But the biblical timeline says 2000 years roughly seventy years compared to even just 2000 years is nothing."

We both get up and we walk to the next booth in the line. The next country was France and the menu was Escargot spread on a baguette with Bordeaux Merlot. "Je Vous Remercie," Megan says to the man behind the counter.

"I get that but what does that have to do with Autism becoming so common in the last few decades." Blaine asks Megan.

"You have to put together the whole picture. Humans have been around hunting and gathering and growing crops and surviving in colonies for 5000 years. The Bronze age was literally like 5000 years ago and from 3000 BC to 1000 AD the progression of technology in civilization was minimal."

"I don't think saying minimal is fair. People learned to speak and write and read. They built cities and pyramids and waterways to help grow crops."

"I am not trying to minimize the creation of languages and the creation of mathematics and architecture. What I am saying is that for that 4000 year span there was plenty of time for the human mind to grow, learn and evolve at a comfortable pace to accept the changing world. Now over the last 100 years we have not had that same luxury."

"So you think that technology is what is causing autism? Like through radio waves or something like that?" Blaine asks Megan.

"Well yes and no. Not through radio waves or radiation, I mean that could be the cause of cancer or something but in terms of autism no." Megan explains to Blaine. "Let's try Japan."

We get up again and walk over to the next booth. It was Japan, you ordered Cold frothy ramen noodles and Sake. "Domo" you say to the man behind the counter as we receive our food.

We continue walking while we're exchanging the noodles and the Sake back and forth.

"I think autism is basically just the human brain's way of trying to overcompensate in some ways to make up for having to over process the way our society is rapidly accelerating technologically. I think autism and forms of it is the human brain recognizing that social cues and social interactions are starting to become obsolete in a way. Because of telephones, video chats, text messages etc. you no longer need to be as sharp to pick up on sarcasm or what people are hinting at."

"Yeah, I guess I can see that in a way I guess."

"I also think that applies not just to the human brain lacking in social areas causing autism. I think mental health as a whole is becoming an issue because of it. Anxiety, depression, suicide, all of these things are growing and getting recognized and diagnosed more frequently. Are we really to believe that no one has been depressed or anxious throughout history either?" Megan explains.

"No, it is becoming more talked about and less stigmatized." Blaine says.

"Yes, that may have something to do with it. But the chemical change in the human brain is the bigger problem. We now HAVE to have an understanding of all of this advanced technology. You absolutely need to know how to use all of this technology to succeed in today's world. It is no longer acceptable to be able to grow a crop of vegetables and harvest them by hand and sell them on the side of the street, you will go bankrupt and starve. You need to know how to operate machinery, how to use the internet to sell your products, and how to market your skills online. In return for having to learn all of this and evolve with this crashing and exploding with new information the human brain has to choose what it is willing to let go of. In some people it is flawless social interactions, in others it is regulating receptors and endorphins that alter your moods, in someone else it is their metabolism and their thyroid slowing down."

"So you think the human body is only capable of so much. Because technology and understanding it is so important our bodies are forgetting how to do things that they have been doing for thousands of years?"

"Pretty much, yeah."

"That is crazy."

"Not as crazy as that sign for that Thai food looks."

The next booth was for Thailand. Their menu was spicy red beef curry and Singha beer. We place an order and get an extra beer because the food is supposedly extremely spicy according to the menu. We receive our order and you tell the man behind the table "khàawp khun."

"Okay, I have to ask, how the hell do you know how to speak in all of these different languages?" I ask you.

"You are not very observant Blaine." You point to the sign at the front of the booth with the food menu on it. "Every sign has a pronunciation guide for how to say 'Please' and 'Thank you' on them."

"I'm an idiot" I tell you.

"Blaine, do you know how to knit?" you ask me.

"No."

"Do you know how to build a house?"

"No, why?"

"Do you know how to butcher a cow or a chicken?"

"No, why?"

"Do you know how to pull out your cell phone and get someone to bring you food to your house? Or how to look up instructions on how to cook? It is not essential for you to know how to do those other things in our society anymore. So naturally, you just never learn how to do it. Your brain clears out that space for things it deems more important, things like how to jump, duck, shoot and cycle through the menu in a video game without having to truly think too hard about it."

"You have definitely made your point now Megan."

"Sometimes you just have to speak the language of the locals I guess."

"What the hell does that mean? We both speak English."

"It's an old saying my Father used to tell me."

"What does it mean?"

"It's kind of just saying like use layman's terms or relay information in a way that your audience can relate to."

"Ahh gotcha, like when in Rome do as the Romans do."

"Exactly! If you're in Rome to truly understand the culture and get the experience you are going to take advice from someone who lives it, not a tourist. You are going to speak the language of the locals so to say."

"Are you Cuban by any chance Megan?"

"No, why?"

"The next booth is Cuba, I was hoping that you could help me speak the language because that food looks amazing."

The menu for Cuba is a Cubano sandwich and Cuban Espresso.

"Wait, A Cuban Espresso!?" I exclaim as I read through the details of the drink out loud "Espresso grounds brewed through brown sugar, that exists!?"

"Uno de cada uno por favor" you say to the man behind the table.

"Wait, wait, wait, where is that on the sign?" Blaine asks Megan.

"It's not. Sé un poco de Espanol Blaine." you nonchalantly rattle off your tongue in my direction and I just stare at you waiting for you to translate what you are saying.

The man from behind the table hands you our order with a smile "Para ti hermosa" he tells you.

"Gracias Señor, estoy halagado" you respond to the man.

I am still staring at you waiting for you to tell me what you two are saying.

"You should really learn some Spanish Blaine, that way you wouldn't have to spend the rest of the day wondering if that charming, handsome man asked me on a date or not."

"Well, did he?" I ask you, embarrassed and a little jealous.

"And you definitely wouldn't have to wonder if I told him yes I would be absolutely delighted to go out with him."

I start to feel a rush of dizziness take over my body. "Can we go sit down?" I asked you.

Blaine gets out of the car and he walks around to Megan's door and opens it up. He reaches his hand into the car and Megan grabs it and uses it to pull herself out.

"And that is all that I remember from that day." Blaine tells Megan.

"You really don't remember anything after that at all?" Megan asks Blaine.

"Nothing."

"I began to walk you toward an empty bench nearby and you passed out. I kneeled down beside you to check your breathing and your breathing was getting heavy so I called for help and the paramedics came." Megan explains to Blaine.

Megan looks down at Blaine lying on the ground taking shallow repeated breaths and she leans down beside Blaine as he is unconscious and she takes her phone out of her pocket.
She begins to dial a phone number and puts the phone to her ear.

"Let's start moving forward with the next stage of the plan." Megan says into the phone.

"After that I took you back to my apartment to help care for you. You came to and you are laying on my couch in my living room."

"What the hell happened, where am I?" you asked me as you tried standing up.

"You passed out at the festival Blaine. The paramedics came and they did all kinds of tests on you. They said you must have passed out from heat exhaustion and they asked where I should take you. I told them to bring you to my house and I would take care of you here."

"They didn't take me to the hospital? I barely know you, how would they just let you take me to your house like that?" you were asking me like you were scared of me.

"Well it took a lot of convincing. I told them that I was your girlfriend and we have been together for a long time."

"You could have been anyone, and they just let you take control of my unconscious body and bring me to your apartment?" you say to me very angrily.

"You could thank me, Blaine. I think some gratitude is in order. I have been sitting here putting ice on your neck and feet and making sure you were breathing and comfortable all day."

"What do you mean all day? What time is it?"

"It's eleven Blaine."

"I have been passed out for almost eight hours?"

"Yes."

"Jesus Christ. That doesn't sound like any heat exhaustion that I have ever heard of."

"I don't know what you want me to tell you, Blaine. We ordered food, you felt dizzy, you wanted to sit down, you passed out. There were paramedics there that checked you out. They said you would be fine if you got indoors and laid down and cooled off. I said to bring you back to my apartment where I would take care of you. You are alive, you are well and you are being extremely mean to me for no reason." I began to break down and cry, I thought I was doing the right thing and you started to lash out at me.

I think you realized that you were being really mean and unappreciative of me and apologized "I am sorry, this is all just very strange to me. Do you think that guy at the Cuban stand could have drugged me?" you asked me.

"I guess that could have happened. Do drugs work that fast? I mean we ate a lot of food and drank a lot. We have been walking around all day. Anyone could have drugged you at any point in time if that's what it was." I explained to you trying to calm you down.

Then we stayed up the rest of the night talking about the day that we had.

Chapter Five

Blaine and Megan slip back into their carefully selected outfits for the evening and check themselves in the mirror and head out of their house and into the car on route to the restaurant.

"I really hope they kept our table, I want you to love this place and this date and I hope us being late didn't ruin it."

"Why would us being late ruin it for me? So we might have to wait or sit at a different table, that's not a big deal. After what we both just experienced in that bedroom I don't think anything could ruin this date."

"Yeah but I feel like I kind of sprung the sex onto you and because of it our table might be gone now."

"Blaine please stop worrying so much, really, it is not a big deal if we have to wait or the table is gone. All that matters is that we are going to be there together."

"I think I'm gonna stop and get an energy drink to calm my nerves from 7/11 before we get there, do you want anything? Blaine asks Megan.

"Umm sure, I'll take a sugar free red bull too, I'm not sure how much being pumped full of caffeine is going to calm you down but you can try." Megan sarcastically says to Blaine.

Blaine gets out of the car and heads into the store.

Megan pulls out her cell phone and scrolls through her contacts. She taps the name "Mother" and sends a text.

"We are on our way, sorry we are running late. Blaine couldn't keep his hands off of me."

"That's why we chose you Megan, you are a beautiful woman."

Megan looks up and sees Blaine at the register checking out and looks over at her and smiles, she smiles back at him.

Megan highlights the text conversation and deletes it.

Blaine gets back in the car "They only had these giant red bulls, I hope that's okay."

Megan smiles at Blaine "Sure I can probably make this one last the rest of the month."

"Alright, we got our much needed caffeine, let's go, I'm starving."

Blaine parks in a spot directly in front of the restaurant.

"Usually this whole street is full, it must be our lucky night" Blaine says to Megan.

He gets out of the car and walks around the back and opens Megan's car door.

Blaine and Megan walk into the restaurant, it is an upscale French restaurant that Megan has been hinting about wanting to try ever since the couple had met.

They walk up to the lady waiting at the check in desk.

"Reservation?" she asks them.

"Yes, the name for the reservation is Blaine. I know we are late and I'm sorry something just happened to come up. We will literally take any table that you have open right now if the one that I had reserved is taken."

"I see. Your table is ready now, follow me."

Blaine looks at Megan "Wow that is lucky, I'm surprised they kept the table for us, we're like almost an hour late."

Megan winks at Blaine "I know, weird, huh?"

"Did you have something to do with this?"

"I may have called ahead and told them we were going to be a little late."

The waitress walks them through the front end of the building where the majority of the general public is sitting and through a curtain to a dimly lit room. There are candles on the table and on the walls and there is a faint orchestra type music playing in the background.

Blaine scheduled this dinner months in advance, he knew everything had to be just right for the night. This type of table at this restaurant was not easy to secure and the price tag that went along with it matched it.

Blaine pulls out Megan's chair and she has a seat at the table. He scoots her closer to the table and she turns around and she thanks him.

Blaine's walks to the other side of the table and he takes a seat across from her.

"This place is really nice," Megan tells him.

"I figured we haven't really had a lot of free time to go out lately so why not make it somewhere really nice now that we have a chance."

The waiter comes to the table and brings them a bottle of sparkling water.

"Sir and ma'am, your plates have been pre selected for you as per your request and we promise to bring you the ultimate romantic dining experience. Your appetizer shall be out soon and we hope that you enjoy" the waiter says as he walks away from the table.

"Wow you really pulled out all the stops for this didn't you Blaine?"

"I told you that I wanted to make tonight special. What better way to make a night special for a woman than to completely disregard her opinions and take away from her any say in what she eats or drinks for the night" Blaine playfully tells Megan.

"Judging by the super fancy sparkling water I would say you probably did a good job."

"By the way Blaine, while you were on your way home I called up to the restaurant and I told them to push our reservation back by about an hour."

"They were okay with that? Also how did you know that we would be late?"

"Because I explained to the manager that tonight was a special night and that when you got home I would be waiting for you in the shower, inevitably that would lead to us having a very intimate session of sex either in the shower or on the bed and then I would inquire of you the story of the day that we first met."

"That is oddly specific and I was almost starting to buy your story until you got into all of the details."

"No seriously, the manager of this restaurant is a woman and I explained everything to her, every single detail and she completely understood. She told me to make sure that we take our time and come here completely relaxed and carefree so that we could enjoy our night."

Blaine stares at Megan for a second "I'm not good enough for you and I don't know If I'll ever be good enough for you."

"Oh shut up Blaine."

"Megan, we've been together for a very long time. I know you are wondering when I plan on proposing. I know that and I am sorry that I have taken this long. I am just extremely fucked up from things in my past. I have been working on getting past all of that and you are the best thing that has ever happened to me. It is only because of you that I think I am even still here today. My life was on a really horrible path before I met you. I've wanted to tell you for a long time but the timing never seemed right."

"I know all of that Blaine, I am not rushing you. I'm just really surprised that was the subject matter you decided to bring up as soon as we sat down,"

"No, no, listen Megan I am sorry. I think maybe after I explain to you all that is wrong with me, maybe you will have a better

understanding of who I am. If you decide you want to leave then I will completely understand. I don't really even know where to start. I know I 've told you my name is Blaine Tyler and if you married me that's the name you'd take if you wanted to take my name."

"So that is not really your name?"

"My name is actually Blaine Tyler Holly. Well my birth name was Blaine Tyler Acadia. I just kept my middle name because it was the only other constant in my life since birth.

My parents adopted me when I was ten years old and they changed my name."

"So you were adopted? That really isn't that big of a deal. That isn't something that you need to be ashamed of or anything Blaine, there are thousands if not millions of people that have been adopted and are perfectly normal and good, productive members of society."

The waiter brings out a plate of charcuterie and escargot and sets it on the table.

"I hope you both enjoy it," the waiter tells them as he walks away again to the back.

"So? You were adopted Blaine, is that it? That's the big shocker to your life story? I'm sorry I'm not more appalled or terrified, I guess I'm not sure of which response you were looking to get out of me. Blaine if this is your way of breaking up with me or like lowering my expectations softly then just do it. You don't have to take me out to this super fancy restaurant to let me down and soften the blow. You know that I am not that kind of girl."

"No! No Megan, that's not it at all. Leaving you is the absolute last thing on my mind, that is the last thing that this dinner was supposed to be about. Let me just start from the beginning, I want you to understand why I've been so slow moving on all of the steps in our relationship."

"Fine, go ahead Blaine. Tell me why."

"It all really happened about four years ago now. That's when everything started to spiral downward for me."

Blaine waves the waiter over and he asks him to bring them a bottle of wine.

"You might want to have a glass of wine or two while I tell you this. It's all kind of a long and fucked up story Megan."

"Well now you really have me interested, and still slightly perturbed. I hope you're not trying to get me drunk just so you can take advantage of me later and kick me out in the morning. After that little introduction you gave me I think there's a chance you might be in the doghouse for a few nights."

Chapter Six

I was sitting at my desk pretending to be looking through files on my laptop. My desk was made of that cheap particle board covered in some type of faux plastic wrap. It was the typical shitty desk you would find in every office building in the world when a business opens up, they must get a pretty great deal on these shitty desks because everyone has one it seems.

I had an impending deadline for a presentation due in the next couple of days about phishing and email fraud. When it comes to large companies like the one that I work for, the topic often becomes a very hot issue. It seems that the larger a company gets the more susceptible they are to being compromised.

Is it because they have more employees and the chances of some dumbass doing something stupid grows or do they just become an easy target because of their growth?

My presentation would tell you that company cyber security is compromised in the majority of cases because of novice users clicking links and opening emails they have no business opening.

The internet has been around and widely available at that point for over twenty years. It was not a new toy, why are people so ignorant towards its capabilities still?

People approach the internet with an uncharacteristic amount of positivity and trust. People who wouldn't normally approach a person on the street and say hello to them then they log onto a computer and they all of a sudden want to welcome them into their lives via social media.

It seems as if these people were to receive a letter in the mail from a company or a person that they were unsure of then they would either shred it or throw it away. That is the normal thing to do, especially in a day and age where anthrax and other poisons are being mailed to people on a regular basis.

However, on the internet they just open the mail and follow whatever link is contained. Without any regard for their personal safety or the safety of the computers they are using.

On the internet all common sense is disregarded it seems. People are much more brave, they are much more adventurous, they are willing to sample a little bit of everything.

I myself was truly no exception either when it comes to the internet.

I knew that I was possibly contributing to a security breach by using a proxy server to access a torrent website and pirating a movie on my work laptop nearly every single day but I was in charge of everything so I know how to cover for myself if anything were to happen.

I at least had the decency to put my web browser into incognito mode and delete my history after I did these things.

I heard my phone ringing and I picked it up and looked at it, it was my Mom.

My Mother and Father are both retired police officers, well they were. My Mother was a police officer for only a few years

in her twenties and that's how she met my Father, my Father stuck with the job a little longer.

She says she quit the job when I was born because she couldn't stand it if I lost both of my parents to that line of work. It is a dangerous job and after doing it for a handful of years she had encountered more close calls than she was truly comfortable with.

She would explain to me that was not the kind of world that she wanted to bring a child into. I needed stability and I needed certainty that I could count on my Mother being there for me as long as possible. She wanted her son to know that he could come home after school and my Mother would be there waiting for him. She would be there to make me lunch and put me to bed.

She would be there for my high school and college graduations, she would be there to take pictures of me at my prom, she would be there at my wedding.

She told me all of that several times throughout my life and she lived up to all of the promises. She never missed a single day or event that was meaningful to me. She didn't want her son to have to grow up an orphan after both of his parents were killed trying to stop gangbangers and low lives. She would tell me that she loved her son more than anything and she wasn't willing to risk her life and mine to try and protect the general public from themselves.

My Father was forced to retire after he was shot after he responded to a domestic abuse call. The irony is that it was the wife that shot him. It was the woman that he went there to protect. He was only 33 years old when it happened but I didn't really remember anything from before when it happened, I can only remember the stories.

It's fairly obvious that I didn't inherit a whole lot from them except for my last name. They were both extremely outgoing, adventurous, motivated and extroverted. I am very much an introvert. I am frequently nervous, anxious and not very social.

But anyway, I knew that she wasn't calling me just to say hi or anything, I'm sure she just wanted me to come by and perform some kind of task for her. I don't mind performing these little odd jobs around her house but my Father lives there too, he is fully capable of doing those things as well you know?

Why does she always have to bother me with her household chores instead of my father? I would ask myself. It was like she didn't choose to marry him, but she chose to give birth to me so why was I always in debt to her?

She married my Father because she saw something in him. She saw a man she could build a family and a home with, a man who could perform small odd jobs and meaningless tasks for her.

My Father told me that she likes having me do them because it gives her a reason to make me come over every now and then. She isn't doing it because she wants to make me work or because I owe her anything. She thinks that by telling me she needs help that I will feel obligated to come over.

Just inviting me over for dinner or to talk had never done the trick to entice me into stopping by. I know this all sounds shitty to me.

It's not that I hated going over there to see my parents or disliked it even really, it's just that I spent twenty years of my life in that house. Now I just preferred being away from it.

I like having my own privacy and my own life away from them.

I knew that my parents wouldn't be around forever and I know that I should have appreciated the time that I had left with them but it's not like they're dying tomorrow I always told myself.

As far as I know, they are more than likely in better health than I am. They are more than capable of going on vacation several times a year, they go to spin classes together, they take walks together every night, they take care of themselves much better than I do and it's obvious.

Every night they are sitting down together at the dinner table and eating a nice, healthy, home cooked meal. They are getting proper servings of fruits and vegetables, they are following the antiquated food pyramid to a tee and they are probably the healthiest people that I know.

I, on the other hand, was eating cold raviolis straight from the can for dinner. I get the majority of my vegetables in the form of pizza sauce. I get my servings of fruit from whatever percentage of fruit comes in energy drinks and pop, most likely zero. The only food pyramid I see are tortilla chips.

I know all of this about my parents. But I know that my Mother probably hounds me just because she misses me and she wants the best for me.

I tell myself that it is the dynamic between almost every normal Mother and son.

So I decided to answer the phone.

"Blaine, your Father and I have decided that we want to sell the house. So would you be able to come by tonight or tomorrow and come help sort through some things in the garage? We want to have a yard sale and get rid of a bunch of things in there. We've found some of those really nice condos nearby and we just won't have the room anymore" she asks me.

I grew up in that house and they didn't even think of consulting me before making a life changing decision like that? I spent almost all of my life in that house. I got my first kiss in that house. I had sex for the first time in that house. I lost my teeth as a child in that house. I was potty trained in that house. I learned to ride a bike there.

Yet no one thought to ask me if I had any input?

"Yeah no problem Mom, I have a lot of stuff over there I haven't seen in years, I 'd like to look through." I told her.

"Don't get all sentimental, most of that stuff you haven't seen in fifteen years because you don't want or need it, just help your Father move everything into the yard, I love you and I 'll see you tomorrow."

"Love you too, Mom."

I knew she didn't want me to actually help look for anything. She just wanted me to move everything out for her. I really don't mind doing it, I just wanted her to tell me that's what she truly wants from me you know?

The biggest fault in the relationship I had with my parents was communication.

But I am sure that if you asked anybody they would more than likely give you that exact same answer.

Are children really supposed to have that type of open relationship with their parents where they can talk to them about everything? I feel like if I didn't want all the details from them about their personal lives they probably wouldn't want to hear about me.

Which really isn't true, any decent parent will always give their child more than enough time to hear about their day. But nonetheless I agreed to help my parents with the task.

I was sure there's a gold mine of late nineties and early two thousand memorabilia in there. Plush toys, Yo-Yo's, video games, pogo sticks, Pokémon cards, all the good stuff. I thought hell, this might be sort of fun after all.

I spent the rest of the day at work going back and forth between watching tv shows and assembling a slide show for the presentation. I knew that no matter what I presented to those people everyone was going to use the internet as they pleased.

People are going to get emails from Nigerian princes asking for money and they are going to open them. People are going to access restricted websites on purpose or by accident that lead to malware being installed on the computers. People are going to access their personal emails at work and their business emails at home. People are going to upload all of their credit card information on websites under the businesses network making them susceptible to a data breach.

These are all things that I have encountered a hundred times and nothing will ever change.

Chapter Seven

Megan is picking through some cheese and crackers as she intently keeps listening to what Blaine is telling her. This is one of the main reasons that he loves her, she is a great listener. Blaine can tell she is interested in everything he is telling her but she is waiting for him to get to the parts that would explain his most obvious faults.

"Try this pickled cucumber" she tells him as she reaches across the table and waves it in his face.

"I believe that is just called a pickle," Blaine says as he takes a bite of it.

"Yeah but this is like a freshly sliced cucumber that's been pickled, it's different, it is so good. Sorry, sorry go on."

Blaine continues telling her his story.

I finish my work day and I make the drive home to change into some clothes that I don't mind getting a little dirty. I have recently seen the inside of my parents garage and I know it's not going to be a clean task.

I think I picked out some sweatpants and an old t-shirt or something, anyway that's not really important. I just didn't want to ruin my good work clothes.

I get back in my car and I head over to my parents house. At that point it was only a mile or two away from me.

Mother really wouldn't let me live much further away from her. I remember that I stopped by a fast food restaurant on the way and ordered the smallest item possible, a small french fry I think it was.

I was not really hungry. I just needed a prop to bring with me to prove that I 've already eaten and a bag is perfect for that. I know that my Mother is going to ask me to stay for dinner and I am really not feeling up to it.

I get to my parents house and my Mother is waiting at the door just like she always is, it's like she had some kind of sixth or seventh sense for when I was near. She comments on me ruining my dinner with that kind of junk food.

Mother wraps her arms around me and she pulls me in close for a hug.

"I missed you honey."

She grabs me by the hand and leads me into the house. She walked me past the bathroom to the right as I entered and we turned left and she led me into the dining room.

"Get yourself a snack and something to drink. That junk food isn't going to hold you over until dinner."

She absolutely hated when I ate fast food, just like you do.

"Sorry Mother I was starving and I couldn't wait any longer." I told her.

"You knew I would be cooking, I 'm sure you and your Father will work up an appetite working out in that garage" she tries her best to guilt trip me.

"We'll see Mother" I tell her as I have grown to become immune to her little guilt trips.

I leave the conversation at that hoping that will be enough to keep her from pestering me for the rest of the time that I am over. I head out into the garage where my Father has been waiting for me and as I enter the door into the garage my Father hands me a beer.

"Thanks bud for stopping by, I told your Mother I was going to do this on my own but she thought you might want to look through some of this old stuff. She kept talking about how me and you need to bond more" Father tells me.

"I'm almost thirty, I think that ship has sailed at this point."

They both share a laugh as they sip on their beers together.

"Damn the garage is a mess, how the hell did I let it get like this?" Father asks as he and I start walking towards a pile of boxes near the front of the garage.

Father and I are searching through everything in the garage while Mother is making dinner inside and cleaning up the house.

She occasionally peeks her head through the side door to the garage and asks us if we need anything from her. That is such a Mother thing to do.

"Are you boys hungry or thirsty? She asks us constantly.

"No honey, we're fine," Father tells her.

"No Mom, I'm fine."

"Well if you need anything please just ask or come get it. You used to live here Blaine, don't act like a stranger in this house" she tells me as she goes back inside.

"Are you staying for dinner tonight Buddy?" Father asks me.

"Probably not, I have a big work project I have to get done by tomorrow morning and I've really been putting it off" I explained to him.

"I don't care but it really hurts your Mom's feelings that you don't spend much time over here these days." Father tells me.

"Can we please just sort through the stuff?"

"I know there should be more of my stuff in here" I say as I am throwing aside boxes labeled 'Kitchen and Bathroom stuff.'

Just like I thought, I found a box labeled 'Blaine's room.' Inside of the box are Yo-Yo's, playing cards, toy cars and a bunch of other small things I vaguely remember playing with.

I continue searching through some more boxes full of pictures, books and old clothes.

"No shit" I heard Father say to himself. "I wonder if this old thing even works still?"

I looked over at him "What did you find?" I ask.

"Isn't this your old computer buddy? I remember when we first bought you the thing. You didn't leave your room for days. You

probably spent 12 hours a day, everyday for ten years on that old piece of crap."

I can't believe it, I had so many good memories with that computer.

"I'm definitely taking this home with me."

I pick up the computer modem and the keyboard and walk it out of the garage and load it up into the trunk of my car with plans on plugging it in, booting it up and looking through all of my old stuff on there later tonight after I get it all home.

Father follows behind me with the monitor, the mouse and all of the extra cords and hands them to me and I throw them into the trunk with the rest of the computer stuff.

"Blaine what the hell are you going to do with that old thing?" Father asks "I'm sure that thing doesn't even work anymore, it's been out here for at least ten years. Through all of the seasons, through the rain, through the cold, the heat, everything. You might as well just throw it away."

"It might not but if it does I 'd love to see all of my old pictures, listen to my old music, and read through my old school work and I would love to just browse through whatever else is on there" I explain to Father .

"You are wasting your time buddy. But if anyone could fix that old thing I 'm sure it's you. At least it's something to keep you happy and busy for a little while" Father replies.

Father and I walk back into the garage and continue sorting through everything else that's been rotting away in the garage. Father and I sort through what is going in the trash and everything that's going to be sold and set everything out on tables in the driveway for my parents garage sale.

Mother comes out of the house to the driveway and thanks me and asks me to stay for dinner just like I thought she would but I make up an excuse as to why I needed to get home.

"I really can't tonight Mother, I have a lot of work I have to get done tonight. There's a big presentation coming up that's extremely important and I really need to devote all of my free time to that today; plus I already ate."

"All you had to eat was that garbage fast food, your brain can't function properly with that in your stomach. You need some real food if you want to do some real work. Fruits and vegetables, not just some deep fried potatoes and fruit flavored pops."

"I'm really not hungry, Mother."

I tell her that knowing that she really just wants to have me sit down with them and catch up, the food is just a means to an end. What I really want is to get home to look through my old computer and be left alone.

Part of me is secretly hoping that there might be some old sexy pictures of my ex girlfriends scantily clad and posing for me. Or maybe even some sexually explicit old email chains between us.

I wonder to myself, "Could I get in trouble if there's nudity on here? I know I 'm an adult now but those would have been taken when I was fourteen. If there is, am I some kind of pedophile?"

I quickly shifted my mindset from curiosity about seeing those old pictures and emails to dead set determination on getting rid of any possible evidence that could be interpreted as criminal materials.

"I promise you I will try my best to stop by again in the next few days. Maybe I 'll come by and help out with the garage sale. When do you plan on having it? Or do you just plan on letting all of the stuff sit outside until the trash guys pick it up or the city fines you?"

We're just gonna let people come by as they want and take whatever they see for free. We have no use for it, whatever doesn't get taken we'll probably just throw it away.

"Well then I guess it's a good thing I already took all of the stuff out of there that I really wanted."

My Mother kisses me on the cheek. "Please try to come by more often Blaine, you know we won't be around forever."

Father gives me a hug and I get in my car.

I roll down my window and look over at my parents. "I know Mother I promise. I will make it a point to stop by again soon and just hang out. I'll call you soon."

I roll my window up and I take off down the street.

I raced home and I couldn't wait to plug the computer in.

I must have been driving suspiciously because about a mile down the road I got pulled over by an unmarked police car. He turned his lights on and drove behind me for a few seconds before I stopped. He sat behind my car for five or six minutes before he got out of the car. I assumed he was just running my license plates. When he approached my car

Don't Shoot The Harbinger

he signaled for me to roll down my window and when I did
he had his gun drawn on me.

He told me that I was speeding, I ran through a stop sign
and I made a turn without signaling. He asked me if I
noticed the old lady a few blocks back crossing the street
that I almost hit. I told him there was no lady and there was
no way that he could have been following me that long
because I had just left my parents house a few streets away.
I wasn't really paying that close of attention to him behind
me though so I couldn't be completely sure.

With everything that had been going on in the world with
police brutality and innocent people being killed during
meaningless traffic stops I wasn't going to debate with the
guy. So I kept my hands on my steering wheel and I just
stared forward as the guy kept waving his gun in my face
and berating me about how irresponsible I was. He took my
license and went back to his car for another minute and
when he came back he threw a piece of paper and my
license at me through my window.

After all of that, I got a ticket for speeding, that's still the
only ticket I've ever gotten in my life to this day and when
I went to court to fight it not only did the officer never
show up they told me that there was never even an officer
that worked there by that name.

Chapter Eight

Megan is still picking through the charcuterie board, picking up cheeses, fruits and different types of breads, looking at them and setting them back and her curiosity eventually has found her way to the escargot.

"What are these exactly?" she asks Blaine.

"Escargot. They are snails. Edible snails cooked in butter. They're actually really good."

She gives him a look of disgust.

"Just try them."

She takes a bite of the escargot and Blaine keeps telling her the story as the look on her face turns from intrigue and caution to pleasant surprise and enjoyment.

Once I got home I set up the computer on the coffee table in my living room in front of the couch. I ran an extension cord from the wall to the computer. I hooked up the modem and the monitor and I plugged them in. I find the mouse and connect it to the modem and I pick up the keyboard, give it a shake and plug it into the back of the modem. I put the power cords in the back of the monitor and the modem and I plugged them into the extension cord I ran from the wall.

I press the power button on the monitor and the modem and the modem takes forever to load up. The screen turns on almost immediately and that gives me a load of hope that all of this may still work properly.

The modem begins making grinding noises and weird beeping noises he's never heard before and the fan kicks on. The fan is running extremely hard and fast, probably because of its age and due to the fact of how long it's been sitting around unused in the garage open to the elements.

The loading screen comes up and I click on my profile, I click log on and just like that my home screen comes up.

I stand by for a minute or two while all of my old desktop items and folders begin to load.

"I can't believe all of the stuff is still here!"

I locate the icon labeled 'My photos' on my desktop and click on it. I browse the folder thoroughly making sure there's no underage nipples, butts, panties or anything that could possibly earn me a prison sentence.

Nothing vulgar, nothing explicit, nothing pornographic, it's safe, I am a little more relieved now.

I continue looking through all of my old music and video files. Senses Fail, The Beautiful Mistake, Brand New, Silverstein all of my old favorites are still there.

I am hit by a huge wave of nostalgia as I flash back to being a teenager sitting in chat rooms all day listening to my old favorite song 'Light A Match For I Deserve To Burn'

Right on my home screen I see a shortcut to my old favorite Instant Messenger program. I clicked on it and all of my old login information is still there.

XxBlaineDamage88xX ... what a stupid messenger name.

"There is no possible way that all of this can still work" I think to myself.

I click login and nothing happens.

"That's because your old computer didn't have Wi-Fi right" Megan chimes in.

"Exactly" I tell her.

So I sort through my closets looking for an Ethernet cord that I can run from my router to the computer, luckily I had about ten of them just lying around.

I set it up to get access to the internet and sit back down. I click login and all of my old friends list appears. I look through all of my old away messages and I get a laugh at a few of them.

I can especially remember using one of them on a regular basis:

"I try to reach your outstretched hands ...oh why do I ? I try. I fail you."

That was some of the lyrics from my favorite song by The Beautiful Mistake.

I guess you could say that I was sort of an emo kid, but that was a phase that I eventually grew out of but the music stuck with me throughout the years as you definitely have heard. Never like feathered black hair and eyeliner emo, more like tight jeans and band shirts emo.

"Oh ha-ha I can definitely picture that" Megan says,

I hear the sound of a door opening and I see that a friend is now online.

"Who the hell uses this still?!?" I laugh out loud to myself.

I got an instant message.

It was from someone named SoccerDude2k1.

SoccerDude2k1:I ! Wow you haven't been on here in forever
xXBlaineDamage88Xx:Who is this again?
SoccerDude2k1:You don't remember me? :(
XxBlaineDamage88xX:No, sorry man I don't.
SoccerDude2k1:Aww :(that's too bad, want me to refresh your memory?
XxBlaineDamage88xX:Umm sure.

I am getting sent a picture file, it's loading.

It pops up and it's a picture of a man naked from the waist down sitting at a computer desk.

I responded back to them.

XxBlaineDamage88xX:Who the fuck is the and what the fuck do you think you're doing?
SoccerDude2k1:Haha you remember now don't you ;)
XxBlaineDamage88xX:DON'T YOU EVER FUCKING MESSAGE ME AGAIN YOU PERVERT!
SoccerDude2k1:You used to love these conversations Blaine.
SoccerDude2k1:What's wrong, you don't like me anymore? :(
XxBlaineDamage88xX:That's it you fucking pervert I'm reporting you to the cops.

The chat window goes silent for a minute before it pops back up.

SoccerDude2k1:You don't want to do that, Blaine.

Another picture begins to load. It's screenshots from prior chat logs that they had dated from 2002.

I began to skim through the chat logs and I can't believe what I am reading.

SoccerDude2k1 sends me another message.

SoccerDude2k1:You don't remember saying those things to me Blaine? You don't remember sending me those pictures of yourself? You are just as guilty as I am. You created those pictures, all I did was look at them. You are just as guilty as me, you would go to prison just like me. That's creating and distributing child pornography Blaine, think about it.

I was a 13 year old kid and the fucking pedophile took advantage of me. Now all these years later he wants to blackmail me? He was grooming me to become some sick twisted psychopath like him and I forgot all about it. There is no way in hell I was going to let him get away with this, I couldn't let him. I shout out loud at the wall.

I turn off my computer and unplug it from the wall.

"Fuck the guy, fuck the sick freak" I slammed my keyboard on the ground and walked away.

I spent the next several hours doing everything I could to try and forget about the experience.

I take a shower to wash off the dirt from all of the boxes and all of the dead bugs, skin cells and other dirty things in the garage of my parent's house.

I go to my bedroom to get dressed and then walk into the dining room. I opened my laptop that was sitting on the dining room table and ordered a pizza. I walked to the living room, turned on Netflix and plop down on the couch.

I take a look at the computer in disgust and I grab the computer off of the coffee table and set it on the floor. I didn't want that fucking thing anywhere in my line of sight.

I spent a couple minutes browsing through hundreds of titles and genres unable to really calm my mind. I am looking through Netflix, Hulu, Amazon Prime pretty much every streaming service I had and I can't find anything to watch, I am just too scatterbrained to find anything of interest to me.

I hear my doorbell ring.

"The pizza is here already? It's only been like five minutes" I say to myself out loud as I answer the door.

Standing at my door is a man in his early forties probably, he's balding on top of his head and with a long greasy looking ponytail, he is extremely overweight and he has on thick framed glasses. He's wearing a blank gray t-shirt and black sweatpants.

He looks exactly like what you would expect when you think of like a forty year old man who spends all of his time playing video games in his parents basement. The only reason he leaves is because his parents forced him to work a few hours a week to pay for his share of the internet bill.

He digs in the bag and presents me with the pizza box with an eerie grin on his face.

"Blaine. here is your pizza sir" he says.

"Umm, thanks, …. But how'd you know my name?"

"It's on the receipt Blaine" he says and gives a wink to me.

I felt extremely uneasy about that interaction as I handed the driver a five dollar bill as a tip and I shut the door.

"Have a goodnight Blaine damage" he faintly says as I shut the door on him.

"Did he just say what I thought he said?" I think to myself.

I reopen the door and step out onto my porch. I looked down the street for any headlights or taillights but I didn't see anything. Nothing and no one is moving, everything is completely quiet.

I set the pizza box down on my porch and I walked out to the street.

"That isn't funny whoever you are. Come back here and say that to my face you fucking coward" I shout out into the empty streets. "That's what I thought you fucking fat, loser, virgin pussy. Go back to jacking off to pictures of children's dicks in your parents basement" I scream out down the road.

I stand in the street for a few more seconds looking up and down the street to see if I can find the man's silhouette moving at all.

I don't see anything except a pair of headlights coming from far away.

I walk back towards my house and up the stairs of my porch.

I pick the box up and examine the box. There are no names or company logos or anything on it, just a weird circle and triangle looking drawing. I gave the box a shake and I didn't hear anything.

I opened the box and it's empty. I walked to the side of my house and opened the trash can. I threw the pizza box in the trash can and I headed back inside.

Once I get inside I take a look at my old computer sitting on the floor where I left it.

"This isn't a coincidence, it can't be." I try to convince myself

I bend down to pick it up, I carry it over to the hallway closet and throw it inside.

"It looks like I'm not eating fucking pizza tonight I guess" I go into the kitchen to make a bowl of cereal and walk back to the living room to decide on a movie.

I hear another knock on my door.

"Who the hell is that now?"

I walk to the kitchen and I grab a butcher's knife out of the kitchen drawer.

The knocking begins to get louder and faster.

Now the doorbell starts to ring.

I grip the knife in my right hand and fling the door open with my left hand.

"Jeez what the hell are you doing with that knife man?"

It's another pizza delivery man, only this time it's a twenty year old kid in uniform. He's maybe six feet tall with greasy blonde hair and few blemishes on his face. He has a really faint mustache like he's been trying to grow it for twenty years and hasn't had much success up to that point.

"Why the hell would you knock and ring the doorbell like that?" I ask the kid.

"You were taking forever and I was supposed to get off of work like twenty minutes ago dude." the kid tells me.

I stare blankly at the guy and I lower the knife.

"Here's your pizza sir" the kid says to me.

He hands me the pizza and I take it from him and I shut the door.

"No tip!? Thanks a lot you dick" the delivery guy shouts as he walks back to his car.

I open the door and scream an apology to the delivery driver as I watch the driver get back in his car and sped off down the street.

I wanted to tell him about the phantom delivery driver before him that received his tip. I thought about it for about five seconds before I realized how absolutely crazy that would sound.

"See that is a perfectly normal interaction, that is how everything is supposed to happen when you order pizza" I told myself in a calming tone.

"That first guy must have made a mistake. He must have come to the wrong house or something, Blaine Damage was just a coincidence." "After the way I stiffed that kid now I can never order from the place again. But at least I won't have to eat fucking cereal for dinner again tonight I guess" I tell myself.

I examined the box, I opened it up and it's just what I ordered: Pepperoni and banana peppers.

I set the box onto the coffee table where the computer just was and I go into the kitchen, I open the fridge and grab a beer. I open it and chug it and I put the empty bottle on the counter.

I breathe a sigh of relief as my stomach intensely starts to growl.

I grab another beer out of the fridge and I walk back into the living room. I grab a slice of pizza out of the pizza box and take a bite.

I settled back down onto my couch and put on a Netflix comedy special.

I should have just fucking eaten at Mother and Father's house.

Chapter Nine

"That's funny, you still do love ordering Pepperoni and Banana Pepper on your pizza, I still think that's kind of a weird combination, I guess you've just always been weird." Megan tells Blaine.

"That was all that you took away from what I just told you?" Blaine asks Megan.

"Well that and the fact that if I ever try to prank you or something I know that there is a fairly decent chance that I'm going to get stabbed"

"I'm glad you are taking all of this so lightly Megan"

"Oh, stop being so serious Blaine, keep going with your story."

I hear a loud crash coming from what sounds like my kitchen and I am startled awake.

I jumped out of my bed and I grabbed a baseball bat from behind my bedroom door. I rush to the kitchen and I don't see anything, the beer bottle is exactly where I left it and the fridge is completely closed.

I look outside my kitchen window and I think I see a silhouette of someone jumping my fence and running around to the front side of my house where my living room is. I ran out of the kitchen and into the living room. I ran to the front door and made sure that it was locked. I look out of my living room window and I don't see anything. I unlock the door, open the front door and look out to the porch but don't see anything.

I take a step out and I see the same silhouette run out from the bushes around the other side of the house and they take off down the street.

"Get the fuck back here" I shout to the person.

I go back inside and shut the door behind me. I relock the door and look out of the window again. I set the bat down beside the door.

I hear another loud crash coming from my bathroom.

I rush into the bathroom and see the bathroom window is open. I look out of the window and I see someone jumping over my fence behind my house and running away.

I can make out a small description of the person as they are running through my neighbors yard and the flood light comes on.

It is the same person that was at my door earlier.

I looked around my bathroom and taped to my bathroom mirror is a piece of paper. I take the piece of paper off of the mirror and look closely at it. It's a print out of another chat log between me and SoccerDude2k1.

I rip the piece of paper off of the mirror and I start to read through the chat log.

SoccerDude2k1:I am willing to pay you for any pictures you can get me?
XxBlaineDamage88xX: What kind of pictures do you want?
SoccerDude2k1:Boys and girls, naked preferably but underwear will do. I will pay more for nakedness.
XxBlaineDamage88xX: How old do they have to be?
SoccerDude2k1: Well how old are you ?
XxBlaineDamage88xX: I'm twelve you know that.
SoccerDude2k1: We all like looking at you Blaine. So find some around your age then.
XxBlaineDamage88xX: And you will pay me?
SoccerDude2k1: Not only will we pay you, eventually we will let you join our club. Would you like that Blaine? Would you like to be a part of our club?
XxBlaineDamage88xX: Yes! No one around here really likes me. I want to be part of your club!
SoccerDude2k1: Then you know what you have to do.

I storm out of the bathroom with the piece of paper in hand and continue to look around the rest of the house. I go through all of the rooms and make sure that all of the windows are locked, I make sure all of the doors are locked and I head into the kitchen.

I turn on the oven and light the piece of paper on fire and I throw it in the sink. I watch as all of the words on the paper begin to burn away. All that is left of the paper is ash now and I turn the sink on to put out the flames.

I walk back out into the living room and I notice that my old computer is sitting back on top of the coffee table. I know that I threw it in the closest earlier because I was eating pizza right there before I went to sleep.

I pace back and forth for several minutes before I plug the computer in. I stared at the blank screen trying to decide what I should do.

I know that if I log on and confront the man all of this is probably going to escalate. Is that what I really want? But I can't just keep letting the asshole keep messing with him.

I take the computer and throw it back into the closet.

To hell with it, he isn't worth my time. I'll just throw the thing out in the morning and that will be the end of it. I'll call the cops, I'll get a home security system. I'll buy a gun and everything will go away.

I felt better knowing that I had a concrete plan in place.

I walk out of the living room back to the bedroom and lay down.

I am laying in bed trying for several minutes to fall back asleep but the computer keeps flashing through my head. I can't sleep when that is constantly beating into my head.

I get out of bed and walk back into the living room.

I walk over to the closet and I take all of the pieces of the computer back out. I assembled it all again and I plugged it in.

I take a seat on the couch in front of the computer and I log into the instant messenger program.

No one is online.

I sit and stare at my computer for a half hour.

Still nothing.

I decided to finally give up and walk back to my bedroom.

Once I reach my bedroom door I hear the sound of a door opening coming from my computer.

I walked back to the computer and as soon as I sat down I heard a door closing.

SoccerDude2k1 is offline.

I sat there for another few minutes before I gave up again.

I walked away from the computer and once again when I got to my bedroom door I heard the sound of a door opening coming from my computer.

I ran back to the computer to sit down.

I hear the sound of a door closing again.

SoccerDude2k1 is offline.

I bring up my away messages and create a new one.

"I know you were at my house. If I see you on my property again I won't hesitate to fucking kill you. The cops have been called about you trespassing and they are making regular patrols to make sure you don't come back."

My doorbell rings and I jump up.

I opened my front room door and taped to the door is another print out.

I take a close look at the print out.

It's a screenshot.

It's a screenshot of my away message.

On the back there was a symbol that looked like an upside down triangle inside a circle and there was a cross going through it, the same one that was on the pizza box. Only this time with the words "Order of Azoth" written underneath.

BEEP BEEP BEEP

I startle myself awake.

I am laying down on my living room couch and the TV is on. I take a look at my phone and it is 6:30 am.

"Fuck I must have fallen asleep and had a bad dream."

I walk into the kitchen and look in the sink, it's empty.

I walk into my bathroom, and I see nothing out of the ordinary.

I walk into my bedroom, nothing.

I looked in my closet and the computer was sitting there just where I left it.

I get in the shower and get dressed and ready for work.

I make sure that all of the windows in the house are locked and all of the doors are locked.

I walk out to my driveway and get in my car.

Sitting on the passenger seat of my car is a picture.

I pick the picture up and look at it.

It's a picture of me sleeping on my living room couch.

On the bottom of the picture is a note that reads "We had a deal Blaine."

On the back is the same symbol that I saw in my dream with the words Order of Azoth written on the bottom.

I sit inside of my car staring at the picture and reading the note over and over. I go back inside and take the computer out of the closet. I plug in the computer and set it back on the coffee table.

I log onto instant messenger.

SoccerDude2k1 is not online.

I sit down tapping my toes impatiently, nothing happens.

I left the room to go to the bathroom and I heard a door opening sound coming from the computer and ran back to the computer.

SoccerDude2k1 is online.

I wait around for a few minutes waiting to receive a message but nothing comes.

I decided to message him.

XxBlaineDamage88xX:Who the hell are you, why did you come by my house last night?
SoccerDude2k1: You invited us over Blaine.
XxBlaineDamage88xX: No I didn't.
SoccerDude2k1: Yes you did.

I received a picture file. I open it up and it is a screenshot from years ago with him inviting me to meet up.

XxBlaineDamage88xX: That was when I was twelve. That was over fifteen years ago. I'm giving you one warning to leave me alone or something bad is going to happen.
SoccerDude2k1:You wanted it, Blaine. You were my project. You were a loner, no one talked to you and I made

you feel special. You owe this to me, I invested so much time into you and one day you just disappeared. I waited, I watched and I knew one day you'd come back.

I take the computer outside and throw it in the trash.

I get in my car and I head to work.

"So the whole part of the people running around your house was just a dream? Everything about the conversation about you being paid to exploit kids was just a dream? You really didn't do that kind of stuff did you?" Megan asks me.

"I'm getting to all of that. There is a lot to tell, a lot you won't really understand until you hear me out. What I just told you was a dream for the most part but it was like Deja Vu. Everything that happened in that dream was a chain reaction almost it seemed like."

Chapter Ten

"The house Caesar" the waiter says as he slides a plate in front of both Blaine and Megan. "You will find the traditional romaine lettuce, freshly shaved parmesan cheese, our house made croutons which are baked fresh daily and seasoned daily as well as our famous house Caesar dressing."

The waiter looks at Megan "Oh, and I almost forgot" he walks back towards the kitchen doors and reemerges with two wine glasses and a bottle. "Your Riesling wine as well" he says as he pours them both a glass.

"If there is anything else I can do for you, feel free to ask" the waiter encourages them.

"That should be fine for now thank you," Blaine tells him.

The waiter walks back into the kitchen area.

"Where was I?" Blaine asks Megan.

"You were driving to work I think"

My entire drive to work seemed like it flew by in an instant. I couldn't remember anything that I had seen along the way. I don't remember any traffic lights, any restaurants that I passed, I don't remember seeing any cars, I don't remember anything.

All I could see for that whole drive was that person's words flashing through my head over and over "We had a deal Blaine."

"Who does this guy think I am? I am not a twelve year old boy anymore, anything I did back then I can't even remember doing. Did I really promise to join their stupid little cult group?"

I pulled into the parking garage at work and I remember feeling extremely paranoid. I remember driving very slowly looking around the garage as several empty parking spots passed me by. I got out of my car and I looked around at my surroundings several times.

"There's a tracking device on my car, I know it. He followed me here, he had to have" I remember thinking to myself, I was extremely agitated.

I ran my fingers along the bumper of my car and I felt a bump and I dropped down onto my knees and tried to rip it off. I take my car keys and I scratch and scratch at it but it can't get a good look at what it is. I drop onto my back and slide under the car, my spare key is taped under my bumper, I forgot that I put that here.

I continue searching the outside of my car from top to bottom looking for some sort of tracking device.

I wasn't exactly sure what I was looking for but I knew that if I were to come across something that seemed suspicious or out of place that I would absolutely recognize it.

I envisioned seeing a piece of metal similar to the look and feel of a watch battery. I envision a man sitting at home on his computer masturbating to a map of me driving around getting off on knowing exactly where I am going.

The man is a sick bastard.

I searched the inside of my wheels, I opened the hood of my vehicle and searched through the engine, I searched under my wiper blades, I opened my trunk and searched every inch of it and I found nothing.

I see a man wearing a sweat suit and sunglasses walking around the corner about 100 feet away and I get back into my car.

I pulled out of the parking structure and I circled around the block several times. I weave in and out of traffic and take different side streets just to make sure I am not being followed.

I was watching my rear view mirror the whole time when I felt a car had been behind me for a suspicious amount of time. I stopped my car and parked on the street. Once the car passes me I turn around and drive the opposite way, making sure I am not setting a pattern.

Ultimately enough time has passed where I decided that I had not actually been followed and I pulled back into the parking structure.

I cautiously watch everyone getting out of their cars looking for that familiar face. I look in every car at anyone sitting inside and examine every parking spot.

Level one, too many cars, not good enough.

Level two, too many motorcycles, not good enough.

Level three, too many empty spaces, not good enough.

Level five, there's no cars here, that's suspicious.

I drove all the way to the roof of the structure.

"No one will be able to sneak up on me all the way up here" I tell myself.

There are cameras on every corner and there are four exits.

I enter the stairwell from the roof access and begin walking down the stairs. I got down two floors then I heard footsteps coming up the stairs toward me from several floors below.

I froze, I clenched my car keys in my hand and made a fist so that the keys create a makeshift set of spiked brass knuckles.

I see a father and daughter walking up the stairs toward me. They both have ice cream in one hand and the daughter is holding her father's hand. They don't look suspicious but you can never be too sure.

How do I know that the computer man is acting alone? He kept saying words like us and we, I just knew there had to be lots of them.

Who is to say that a father and his little daughter can't be a part of their shitty little cult? They wanted me then I was a kid, maybe they recruited this little girl now as well.

I smile and wave at them. I don't want to come off as too suspicious or equally unwelcoming.

If I get attacked by someone else and the man is the only other person nearby that can help I don't want to burn my bridges. It is a really hard line to walk knowing there are faceless people out there who want to hurt you but not being able to alienate the honest ones who could save you.

The little girl looks up at me and she sheepishly scoots closer into her father, I can identify with that girl.

"It's okay, Kelsey say hi to the young man," the father says to his daughter.

She looks up at me again and her face turns red.

I looked down at her, I knelt down so that I was at eye level with her. I extend my hand out to her.

"Hi Kelsey, I'm Blaine and it's very nice to meet you."

She smiles at me and as soon as she reaches her hand out to shake my hand I hear a car alarm go off.

I immediately stand back up and hurry past the father and daughter, almost knocking the ice cream out of their hands in the process.

"I am so sorry" I say as I try to get to the ground level as quickly as possible.

I am sprinting down four flights of stairs as quickly as possible. I can feel my lungs burning and my ankles and knees are popping with every single step. My thighs are on fire and I trip and fall down several steps and rolls until I hit the landing.

I had another flight of stairs to go.

I get up and look around, there is a group of men standing at the far end of the parking structure staring at me, pointing and laughing.

I brush myself off and hobble down the last flight of stairs.

"If I make it out of the parking structure alive, I swear I will get in shape. I will start running 3 miles every single day."

I reach the ground level of the parking structure and I stop to catch my breath.

I look around to take a quick survey of the immediate surroundings. The ground level of the parking structure is full of cars, but I don't see anyone in the immediate area.

I walk out of the structure and begin heading towards the building I work in. My building is two blocks from the parking structure but I know it's the closest public parking area to where I work.

I notice every single detail about every single person that I passed on that two block walk.

Every person I see approaching me I take a complete and thorough mental assessment of. I looked them up and down, I watched how they walked, I watched their eyes to see if they were hinting at someone sneaking up on me and I watched their hands to see if they had any weapons or anything that could hurt him..

There isn't a single person that I feel I can trust at this point.

Not a single person that crosses my path can be trusted, not a single person that is sitting outside eating at a restaurant can be trusted. Not the homeless people asking for change, not the teenagers skateboarding down the street, not the old women speed walking.

When I finally got to my office I took one last scan of the street and I felt like everyone I had just walked by was either staring at me or talking about him.

I enter the building, walk past the doorman and head toward the elevator. I scan the list of buttons looking for anything out of the ordinary.

I remember reading a story about people putting poison on common public items that leach into your bloodstream and shortly afterwards kills you.

I push the button to the 20th floor.

The elevator opens and there is a woman I recognize exiting.

"Hi Blaine!" She exclaims "Good morning, how are you!?"

"I'm fine." I respond as I slide past her.

She stops in the doorway of the elevator waiting for me to say a little more.

The lady and I have never really had a conversation outside of work that wasn't work related. She chooses now to want to figure out the ins and outs of my life. This is the moment that she chose to try and get to know me a little better, to express her interest in me?

I stare at her and behind her coming through the doors is a familiar face. It's the pizza guy from last night.

"It was good seeing you Karen have a great day, maybe we can go on a date or something some time, alright great, bye again." I nervously say as I begin to repeatedly hit the button to close the elevator doors.

The trip to get to the twentieth floor seems like it is taking hours. This was normally a very fast elevator. I am expecting the elevator to stop and the lights to turn off. I am expecting someone to drop in from the ceiling or to stop at a different floor and have a group of cult members bombard me and kill or kidnap me.

I looked up at the indicator as it blinked on the 20th floor and the intercom announced the floor that I was on.

Usually this is a cool little feature but today the voice can only remind me of what the voice on the other end of my computer probably sounds like.

I imagine the digital elevator woman's voice telling me to join their cult, to help them kill and abduct children and traffic them to sick freaks around the world.

The door to the elevator opens and I can't wait to get out.

I quickly walk into my office and slam the door behind me, when I look at my desk, my boss is sitting there with his feet up and waiting for me.

"You're late Blaine. The presentation is in ten minutes and now we don't have any time to go over it. Looks like you're on your own for the one pal" my boss explains as he playfully laughs.

I have known the guy for years now and I feel like I can momentarily let my guard down.

"Yeah, yeah that's fine. I was up late working on the damn thing, everything will be great."

My boss and I walk together to a conference room nearby.

They set up the projector and get all the documents sorted out and set at every seat.

As they are sorting and passing out the paperwork people begin piling into the room and filling up seats at the table.

I have seen almost everyone before entering the room except for one person. The man takes the last seat. He's wearing a light gray suit, a white dress shirt and a red plaid tie. He is balding on top with a long ponytail, he is extremely overweight and he has on thick framed glasses.

This is the man I just saw in the lobby.

This is the pizza man from last night.

I can tell by the way that the man is staring through me that the man can tell that I know him. I know exactly who he is, but how did he get in here?

Why are all of my co-workers talking to him?`

I spent the next twenty minutes nervously trying to explain cyber security to these men and women in the conference. I am sweating and stuttering, I am falling over my words and I can't help but stare at the man between words.

How am I supposed to give a presentation about cyber security and safety to the one person I can't get away from on the internet?

I stop mid sentence and look at my boss.

If you have any questions, direct them to Mark.

I rushed out of the room, I ran to the elevator, I frantically pushed the button for the ground floor.

The elevator opens up and Karen is standing there again trying to exit.

What are the odds that she would be in my way when I'm trying to get away from the man twice? She has to be part of them, she just has to be.

I aggressively push past Karen as she tries to get out of the elevator and continue their conversation from earlier.

"What the hell Blaine, you fucking jerk, see if I go out with you now" she exclaims.

"I wouldn't date a member of a fucking pedophile cult anyway Karen, stay the fuck away from me!" I shout as the door closes.

The elevator opens and the digital elevator woman's voice says "ground floor Blaine, you can't run forever" as I burst out of the elevator though the building.

I run the two blocks to the parking structure pushing my way through crowds of people that are shouting profanities and threats at me as I go by.

I get to the parking structure and I rush up all the flights of stairs to the roof.

My car is still the only car on top.

I look around and there is no one around, there is nothing around, everything is quiet.

"That couldn't be him in there, there's no way" I try to reassure myself.

I search my car again as quickly as possible for any tracking devices I thinks may have been planted in or on my vehicle

I get in my car and drive home.

The whole way I am comparing the memories of the man in the office to the man from last night. It was dark out and I couldn't get a perfect look at him but I am positive that was him.

I thought I was positive anyway but I really began to question my memories. That is a huge accusation to place on somebody when you aren't 100% sure what you saw.

There's no way that's the same guy. It has to be the same guy. There's hundreds of guys who could look like that. I pulled into my driveway and parked my car.

I take the keys out of the ignition and look around.

"That was not the man from last night, you're crazy, it is just your mind playing tricks on you. Should I call Mark and apologize for storming out like that? There's no way Mark knew that guy he didn't say a single word to him. Is Mark involved too? My own fucking boss is part of a pedophile cult?!"

I get out of my car and take one more look around.

I take a deep breath.

"I need to calm down. It's all in my head. It's all just one big coincidence."

I take out my phone and I text Mark.

Me: Sorry Mark, had a panic attack, had to get out.
Mark: What the hell was that about? You kept staring at the CFO.
Me: The fat guy in the gray suit is the CFO?
Mark: Yeah, you don't remember meeting him before? I specifically requested that you handle that project, that's why he was there, to meet you. There was gonna be a big promotion in it for you if you did well.
Me: Thanks Mark, I'm sorry, I'll make it up to you.

"See, everything is fine, everything is just the way that it's supposed to be. I knew it was all in my head. I have seen that guy before at work, there's no way that was the pizza guy.."

I unlock the door to my house.

I take my shoes off at the door and I go to throw my keys onto the coffee table.

The keys hit something and fall to the ground.

I look over at the keys on the ground and I look up and it's the computer, it's now sitting back on my coffee table.

"I thought I threw that fucking thing in the trash" I think to myself.

Chapter Eleven

Blaine reaches over to Megan and he dabs a napkin to the side of her mouth to wipe away bits of dressing that found its way off of a stray piece of lettuce and onto her mouth.

Megan looks up at Blaine and smiles "Thank you very much."

"So that elevator really told you that you couldn't run forever? Or do you think that you just maybe let everything get to you and you made that little part up in your mind after all of this time?" Megan asks Blaine.

"No, no, no I definitely heard that elevator say that to me on the way out of the building. I know it's crazy but think about it, there has to be someone inside of a security office monitoring all of the movement within the building. Maybe they just got over the speaker in the elevator and have been narrating it this whole time when they see me."

"That is crazy, but when you put it that way it does seem fairly plausible, I'm sure there are speakers all over those buildings that people can make announcements over for emergencies and stuff like that. So you get home and the computer is back on your coffee table that you thought you threw in the trash?"

"No. I KNOW I threw it in the trash, Megan"

I can't believe my eyes, I sit on my couch and my instant messenger screen is already loaded. I look closely at the screen and I have a message from SoccerDude2k1 waiting for my arrival back home. That is another thing that just couldn't be some fabricated thing in my memory.

SoccerDude2k1: You need to message me as soon as you read this. Now that you know how many people we have working together, surely you now know that we are serious. By the way Don says your presentation went well ...except for the parts where you kept stuttering and looking at him while you pissed your pants like a scared child.

"So the man named Don was not the mastermind behind all of this?" Megan asks.

"I wasn't sure at that point I was just wondering if he was just trying to mess with my head even more. I keep talking about how there are tons of them but I 've only ever seen him. The pizza guy and now the CFO of my job was the only face I could put to this group and to that symbol so I had to assume he was behind it all and this was just some ploy to keep me afraid of finding him."

I take a moment to think through my decision and decide if I really want to keep going through with all of this. If I message him back, I'm certain there's no going back. But is there really any turning back at the point anyway?

So I decided to message him back.

xXBlaineDamage88Xx: What are you trying to accomplish?

SoccerDude2k1: We invested a lot of time in you Blaine, and that is time that we want back. We are absolutely going to get back one way or another, we hold all of the cards here Blaine.

xXBlaineDamage88Xx: I have no idea what you are talking about.

SoccerDude2k1: Don't you play stupid with me. You know exactly what I am talking about. The only reason you aren't in prison right now is because of us.

xXBlaineDamage88Xx: Prison? What do you mean Prison? You are the ones following me. You are the ones breaking into my house, stalking me at my job, sending me threats and lewd pictures.

SoccerDude2k1: Quit playing stupid kid. We protected you during that investigation and you disappeared on us. You are just as guilty as us and you never showed us the respect and appreciation that we deserved.

xXBlaineDamage88Xx: What investigation are you talking about!? Quit playing these games with me, I have no idea who you are.

I start receiving another picture file from this man and it's even more screenshots.

SoccerDude2k1: Is any of this familiar?

I looked closely at the screenshots and it is exactly what I remembered from my dream.

xXBlaineDamage88Xx: I did not get pictures of naked children for anybody. You are fucking with me, you have to have the wrong person.

SoccerDude2k1: You did it Blaine. You loved doing it, you wanted to be a part of the group so bad you were willing to do anything for us.
xXBlaineDamage88Xx: I would never do anything like that. That is disgusting, you are disgusting.
SoccerDude2k1: If I am disgusting, then what are you? You are the disgusting kid who would do absolutely anything in the world to be a part of this group.

I started receiving another picture file, only this time it is a picture of a child. I started receiving picture after picture from him. Every single picture he sends is worse than the last. Every picture is more disgusting, more indecent, more horrific. Every picture I receive is more and more vile until I can't take it anymore.

xXBlaineDamage88Xx: I really did that to these children? There is no way I could have done that. I am a good person, I would never do that.
SoccerDude2k1: You did, and you loved doing it. You made a lot of money for us . There are a lot of people out there who pay big money for that kind of stuff. It is not about good and evil or being bad or decent Blaine, this goes much deeper than that. We are powerful, you are powerful, we are rich and we are untouchable. We don't do these things for pleasure, we do them because we can and because people want it. If this is a demand for a certain product we will provide it and that product comes with a steep price.
xXBlaineDamage88Xx: That is disgusting.
SoccerDude2k1: Is it more disgusting that they receive pleasure by looking at those images or is it more disgusting that you received money for selling those images that you

obtained? You exploited all of your little friends Blaine and you did it for years.

I have to step away from my computer and recompose myself. There is absolutely no way that I could have done that. I am not the type of person who would do something like that. There is no way I could do that.

"Could I really do that? Am I really capable of being that kind of monster? If I did I was just a kid myself ... I didn't know any better." I ask myself.

xXBlaineDamage88Xx: What did you mean that I could be in prison and you protected me?
SoccerDude2k1: I will show you.

He sends me a link to a website.

It redirects me to a news article about a government bust of a child pornography ring. I skimmed through the article looking for any names that I might recognize. Mick Merino, Pat Lichot, Mike Szolnok, none of those sound familiar.

I keep skimming through the article looking for any mention of my name.

I finally came across the section that I had been looking for.

"One minor child's computer was confiscated in the raid but due to the age of the suspected offender their name cannot be released. Hundreds of pictures and videos were found to be distributed between the users over the course of several months. Each person found guilty can face up to forty years in prison for their crimes."

I message the man back.

xXBlaineDamage88Xx: If all of this is true then why are you coming after me now?
SoccerDude2k1: You logged onto the program Blaine. You know what we used this for. Why else would you log in after all of these years? We thought you wanted back in.
xXBlaineDamage88Xx: I just found the computer in my parent's garage, I don't even remember any of it.
SoccerDude2k1: Your parents took you away from us Blaine. We groomed you, we made you into the man that you are today. You spent eleven years with them and you were never happy. You spent one year with us and you loved your life. You belong with us Blaine.
xXBlaineDamage88Xx: I need time to think about this. I just need some time to process everything.
SoccerDude2k1: We will be watching you Blaine to make sure you don't do anything you might regret.
xXBlaineDamage88Xx: I won't, I just need to piece all of this together.

I sign off of Instant Messenger and there is a knock on my door.

I stand up quickly and rush to the door. I open the door and look outside but I don't see anybody. There is a box sitting on my porch.

"Should I really open the thing?" I think to myself.

I brought the box inside of the house and I opened the box. Inside of the box is a brand new laptop with a note attached to it that reads: "We've been waiting for you to come back." I put the laptop back in the box and walked it outside and threw it in my trash can.

I hoped that there was someone out on the street watching me. I want them to see me throw it away.

"I know you can see me, fuck you and fuck your pervert cult." I shout out into the street as I storm back inside of the house and slam the door behind me.

I know that there is no chance in hell that I am going to join the cult of pedophiles. I need to figure out a way to find out who some of them are so I can locate them and turn them over to the FBI or the local police department or dateline NBC. I had to expose them to someone.

I open up my laptop and enter the names of the men from the online article in a search engine.

All of the men that were involved are still in prison. All of their mugshots are found online with descriptions of the crimes they committed:

Manufacturing Child Pornography.
Possession and Distribution of Child Pornography.
Coercion or enticement of a minor via the internet.

A few of them even have Criminal Sexual Misconduct charges from then, I guess that they decided that just trading videos wasn't enough for them anymore.

Trying to find one of these guys isn't going to be any help while they're sitting in prison, hopefully getting beaten and raped every single day of their lives.

I get an idea on how to start finding all of these sick perverts and I know exactly who to start with.

I remotely log onto the computer system at work and get into the camera system. I rewind footage from earlier in the day to find the guy from the presentation room. What did Soccer dude call him? That can't be a real name? Don? I find the guy and I track my movement from the presentation room to the elevator to the front door of the building moving in reverse.

I switch the cameras from the inside of the building to the outside of the building. I watch the man walk down the street several blocks and he is coming from a parking structure, it's the same parking structure I was in.

I rewind further and further back to when I pulled out of the parking structure and drove towards the building and started going in circles to lose whoever was following me. There was a blue sedan that was following close behind me the whole time. I was relieved to reaffirm that I wasn't crazy, I knew I was being followed in that parking structure and I knew I was being followed while I was driving.

I zoom in on the car and I can sort of make out the driver of the car. It looks like me but I can't be 100% sure.

But on the front of the car clear as day is a license plate number.

ADK7823.

I knew that I had him now.

Chapter Twelve

Megan and Blaine have both finished their salads and they have their plates set off to the side to be picked up by the waiter. They are both finishing off their glasses of wine the waiter had brought out earlier.

"Is it really that easy to just look people up on the internet?" Megan asks Blaine. "Like to just get someone's license plate number then track where they live and all of that information about them?"

"Absolutely, all you really need is a little bit of information on someone and you can find pretty much anything about them if you really want to. It is truly kind of scary that someone can find out about you with just something small like your name if they know what they are doing. When you have something even more specific like a license plate number, there is absolutely no hiding from that. All of your information is entered into government databases which are pretty easy to access. Even more so beyond that, all of the privacy agreements you enter into on social media or YouTube gather all of that private information too and compile it together."

"And you were the kid whose computer was taken during this raid of this child sex and pornography ring? What exactly did you do?"

"I'm getting all of that babe, this is where you really just need to have an open mind and hear me out because it gets extremely fucked up. But you will hopefully see that I was just some dumb a naive kid who was being taken advantage of."

"I will try to just listen and understand but where this seems to be heading, I can't make any promises, this all seems just like extremely, EXTREMELY messed up."

ADK7823 is his license plate number. You never really think that people like him live normal lives. They go grocery shopping, they pay the bills, they pay taxes, they have to go sit in the DMV to get their license plate numbers assigned to them.

It's sort of like when you are a kid and you see a teacher outside of school for the first time, I guess.

ADK7823, that should be easy enough to find.

Luckily the state we lived in had an online database registry of every license plate number. You can look it up and find the name, address and date of birth of anyone.

Our society is making it nearly impossible to have any anonymity. But what can you expect when everyone has ten social media accounts, each with their face uploaded onto it dozens of times over.

Donald Mabury, 6754 Elm Buffalo Grove IL.

I entered it into my phone and it was only a 15 mile drive away from him. I made the drive from my house to Buffalo

Grove via Lake Cook Road, not that you really know any of that but it was really just one straight shot for me to get there.

I was not sure what to expect when I got there, I'm not even sure what my plan is when I do get there or what I'm going to need so I stopped at a hardware store on the way to hopefully give me some ideas.

I spent about a half hour walking back and forth through the aisles looking at everything. I was trying to remember what I had seen on T.V in crime shows.

I grab rope, duct tape, a razor knife, a plunger and plastic drop cloth.

I look in my cart and I think it looks suspiciously like what someone who is about to kidnap and torture would buy. Is that what I plan on doing? Kidnap and torture? Either way if it is I can't be so obvious.

I grabbed a bucket of paint, some brushes and some caulk just to complete the look of someone who is remodeling. I throw them all in my cart and take them to the checkout line.

I looked around nervously hoping that I hadn't been followed since I left my house. I had spent the last hour trying to formulate a plan that I had completely forgotten that I had been followed every second for the last day of my life.

134

If anyone has seen me buying the stuff they would have to know that I was up to something. If they saw me they would have alerted everyone of my whereabouts and everyone would be cautious of him.

Maybe I am starting to get too paranoid, I think to myself.

I continue to check out, I pay and throw everything in the trunk of the car. I hadn't noticed anyone coming out behind me or sitting in their cars paying any attention to him. I'm starting to wonder if these people have access to security cameras or traffic cameras and that's how they have been following me so closely.

I turn the GPS on my phone back on and head west towards Elm street. Then it dawns on me "Fuck I'm using my GPS, they will for sure know where I'm heading." I try to memorize the directions and I shut the location on my phone off.

I pull onto Elm Street and I am driving slowly looking for the address. Even numbers are to my right and odd numbers are to my left.

6760, 6758, 6756, there it is 6754.

I make a couple passes by the house to get a better understanding of the layout before I park a few houses down.

It is a typical ranch style house. The gate is on the right side of the house and there is a small fence to the left. The front of the house is covered in bushes. It looks like he pays a good amount of money to ensure that the property is kept properly.

There are no cars in front of the house or in the driveway. The garage is set back behind the house about thirty feet, it's possible that he stores his car in the garage. The lack of visible cars doesn't mean that no one is home. I start to wonder if the man has a wife or children that could be home right now.

I get out of the car and I walk up to the house. I rang the doorbell and I realized what the hell I was doing. "Did I just ring the fucking doorbell?!?" I jumped off of the porch and ran around the left side of the house and jumped over the fence.

I stand at the side of the house waiting to see if anyone comes to answer the door.

I wait and wait but I don't see or hear anything.

There is a window above my head I stand on my tiptoes to look into. The room is empty except for a desk and computer chair, but no computer in sight.

I keep walking until I get to the next window, I look in it and it is the bathroom. The bathroom is empty except for a toilet, a shower and a sink. There's no toilet paper in sight, no hand soap, no towels, the shower doesn't even have a curtain on it.

I walk around the backside of the house and there is a sliding door. I give the sliding door a pull and it is unlocked. I slowly enter through the door and immediately scan the area. I am in the kitchen, the kitchen has no tables, no food sitting on any of the counters, no paper towels or pots and pans sitting out. I open up a couple of the counter drawers and they are completely empty. I open up the fridge and it is empty as well.

To the far left of the room next to the fridge is a staircase going downstairs to a side door and beyond that the stairs continue to what looks like the basement.

Straight ahead looks into the living room. I walk straight forward into the living room making sure to be as quiet as possible. The living room is mostly unfurnished except for a small couch in front of a big bay window where the blinds are closed.

Down the hallway to the right are three doors, one door must be the room with the chair and desk and the other must be the bathroom. I opened both of those doors just to confirm what I thought and I was correct, just an empty bathroom and an almost empty bedroom.

I open up the third door and inside of it is what looks like a makeshift photo studio. There is a camera, a bunch of backdrops on the walls and a green screen. There is a large box full of different props. This must be where they produce some of their filth.

I exit the room and head back into the kitchen towards the basement. I hear noises coming from the basement, I inch down the stairs and slowly and softly as I can and I peak my head around the corner. It was him and he was unknowingly walking towards me. I head back upstairs and stand around the corner.

The man climbs up the stairs and as he gets up to the last step I step around the corner and I ball up my first, I cock it back and I muster up all of my strength as I swing it forward at the man and my punch hits him square in the nose. The man stumbles backward trying to regain his balance on a piece of flat ground behind him that doesn't exist, instead he finds the gap of air between the two stairs and he begins to tumble down the stairs. I run down the stairs behind him and as the man stops his downward descent suddenly the back of his head hits the concrete block wall. At nearly the same time as his head hits the wall I lift my foot and with nearly as much force as the punch I threw I stomp down on the man's head.

The combination of the hard cement wall and the heel of my boot leaves no room for his head to move as the shockwave of force travels through every inch of his brain matter and skull. Although externally his head doesn't budge an inch, internally his brain is sloshing around back and forth in his skull, the blunt force trauma most likely causing a concussion and rendering him to lose consciousness.

I deliver a few more blows to the man's face starting with my feet. Soccer kicks to his face with the point of my toe, downward thrust kicks to the side of his head with my heel then alternates to my fists. I drop down to my knees and I wrap my hands around his throat and I squeeze as hard as I can for a few seconds just to be sure that he stays unconscious.

I ran up the stairs and out of the side door of the house to my car as quickly as possible. I open the trunk and I grab the rope, duct tape and the razor knife and run back into the house.

As I am running back down the stairs to the basement I see the man moving his arms and legs. He braces himself against the wall for stability as he is starting to regain a little bit of awareness and consciousness and tries to get to his feet. I jump on his back and wrap my arms around his neck with my forearm directly over his Adam's apple and squeeze as tight as possible. I wasn't completely sure if this would work but I remember seeing this on TV as a kid and I do my best impersonation of professional wrestlers like 'Stone Cold' Steve Austin and all of those actors and MMA fighters as best as I can. My technique must be decent because the man slips back out of consciousness fairly quickly.

I bend down and tape the man's hands together behind his back. I then tape his feet together and put a piece of tape over his mouth and eyes.

I stand up and walk around the basement looking for a chair to tie the man to. At the bottom of the stairs to the right is a large room with a washer, dryer and a laundry tub. There are a couple steel folding chairs with piles of folded laundry sitting on them. I throw the laundry off of one of the chairs and bring it out.

I set the man up on his butt, I squat behind him and lift him up onto the chair. I grab the rope and tie him to the chair. I've never done this before so I make sure that I use more than enough rope for the job. Just to be extra sure I go around the man several times with duct tape as well.

I continue to walk around the basement to get a better understanding of where I'm at. There is a large bed, a computer desk, a couch and a flat screen TV in a corner of the basement. This must be where the man spends most of his time. A fat, balding pedophile who spends all of his free time in his basement, what a cliché.

I walk back to the laundry room and grab another steel chair. I sit down a few feet and I wait for the man to regain consciousness.

The man starts to wake up and he tries to speak but his mouth is taped shut. He tries to move and he realizes that he is tied and taped to the chair. He tries to look around but his eyes are taped shut.

"Hi, do you know who I am?" I said to him.

The man tries to mumble something but he can't speak.

"I'm going to take the tape off of your mouth but if you try to bite me or spit at me I will put it back on do you understand? Nod yes if you understand" I explained to him.

The man nods his head yes.

I stand up and walk over to the man and remove the tape from his eyes.

The man squints as his eyes adjust to the light and they immediately focus on me and his pupils grow. I remove the tape from his mouth.

"I don't know anything!" the man exclaims.

"Shut up, I didn't tell you to talk" I told him.

"Why are you doing this to me??"

I stand up and pick up my chair. I fold it up and I swing it as hard as I can at the man's face.

CRACK!

The man's chair tips backward and he falls to the ground. The man's nose immediately begins pouring out blood. The man is spitting blood out from his mouth and he is trying to speak.

"I said shut up" I yelled at him. "Why the fuck have you been following me? You came to my house, you came to my work, you have been following me for the last 24 hours and I want to know why."

I stand the man's chair back up so that I can speak to him face to face.

"I haven't done any of those things. I swear it."

"Wrong answer. I saw you. You were on my porch. You were in my bedroom. I saw you on camera in the parking structure. You followed my car. You followed me. Now tell me why."

"It wasn't me" he sarcastically responds to me.

"I can see that it isn't going to go anywhere at this pace."

I grab the razor knife from the floor and walk over to the man. I grab the man's ear and I begin to cut at it until it is completely removed from his head. I remember seeing this from a movie and it got a cop to tell a bunch of things, surely it has to work on this guy.

The man is screaming in pain and blood is pouring from the brand new opening in his head courtesy of me.

"You have another ear, you have a nose, you have a tongue, you have fingers and I have nothing but time. Now tell me why." I scream at the man.

The man is beginning to hyperventilate, breathing harder and harder until he can muster up enough strength to say "Fuck you, I will never tell you anything. You were supposed to be the chosen one. You were supposed to lead us and now look at you, you are nothing. You are a coward, you could have been great" the man tells me.

"What do you mean I was the chosen one? I was supposed to lead you? You are just a group of sick perverted freaks. You exploit children, you profit off of them and their pain. Those children have families and futures and you take all of that away from them. From the looks of your little movie studio you do more than that too."

"You are so naive. We are bigger than that, we are more than that. That isn't even the beginning of what we're capable of. All you've seen is the tip of the iceberg. Now you are fucked, now you are dead, you are dead just like your parents are dead."

As the man said those last words I lunged forward and lodged the razor knife into the man's throat and he began gasping for air. I pulled the knife out and reinserted it into his neck and face a handful of times before I was able to regain control of my mental faculties.

I kick the man's chair over and watch as he starts choking on the blood. The man's blood was spraying from his throat, from his mouth, from his nose, and from his eyes until there was no blood left to leave from his body.

I walk over to the man's computer modem and I pick it up. I walk back towards the stairs and out of the house. I threw the computer modem in the front seat of my car. I open up the trunk of my car and I tear off several pieces of plastic from the roll of drop cloth. I place them on the floorboard of the driver's side of the car as well as the driver's seat.

There has to be some important information on here if that man was willing to die for it.

Chapter Thirteen

Blaine stops talking and he looks intently at Megan to try and gauge a reaction from her. He is surprised that she isn't a lot more bothered or squeamish by the information he just told her.

"Well, how do you feel about me now?" Blaine asks Megan.

"I promised you that I would hear you out and try not to be too judgmental. You killed a child sex predator, that is a little surprising but that is good I guess. At least now I know if we have children in the future there is one less of those kinds of people out there that can hurt them" Megan reassuringly tells Blaine to make him feel better.

The waiter approaches the table and Megan and Blaine both stop their conversation and look up at him. "So sorry to interrupt. Are you ready for the main course?"

They both look at him, they look at each other and nod in agreement. "Yes, we're ready" they say in unison.

"Great, very well, I will be back shortly." The waiter grabs their used plates and disappears to the back again.

Blaine takes what's left in the bottle of wine and pours it evenly between both of their glasses and continues with his story.

"Where was I?" Blaine asks Megan.

"You had the modem in your car and you were covering everything in plastic and I'm assuming you were about to start driving home to check what was on the man's computer."

I drove home and now I am feeling more paranoid and anxious than ever. I had a million thoughts racing through my head. I just killed someone, I just committed manslaughter, that has to change you. If there was ever a reason for this group of people to start following me, that was definitely it.

But they don't know what happened in that house. If this is the guy that's been following me everywhere and tracking my every move then I'm in the clear now. I took care of that problem. He had to be the mastermind behind everything and If I got rid of him and I took his computer then that would just have to be the end of everything.

I check my rear view mirror, I check my driver side mirrors and I don't notice any suspicious vehicles around me. I can finally start to feel relaxed. I know that these people know where I live but I should have some time before they find out what I did. I had at least enough time to get home and wash the blood off of myself, enough time to throw my soiled clothes in a bag and look through the computer.

I foolishly and sophomorically think to myself Hell, maybe then if they find out what I did they'll finally leave me alone. Maybe then I can go back to my salad days before I found out what a human being looked like in their last moment of life. Before I found out that there was a supposed group of elitist pedophiles and human traffickers living all around me.

I pull into my driveway, get out of my car and walk around to the passenger side door. I open the door and grab the man's computer out of the car and carry it inside. I look around me to see if anything out of the ordinary catches my attention.

I bend down and set the modem by the front door.

I walk back outside and remove all of the plastic drop cloth pieces from inside of my car. I take the plastic pieces into the bathroom and throw them into the bathtub to clean off when I get the opportunity. I don't know if there is a more damning piece of evidence than plastic sheets covered in human blood.

I walk back into the living room, take the modem and set the computer modem on the dining room table. I grab my laptop and run an Ethernet cable between the two. I plug the modem in and turn on my laptop. The modem is now displaying onto my laptop screen as it loads up.

I head into the kitchen and grab a trash bag from underneath my sink and carry it with me to the bathroom. I set the trash bag on top of my toilet seat and I get inside of my bathtub and begin to undress. I turn on the showerhead faucet and take every article of clothing off and place them in the tub. I grab the pieces of plastic from the tub and lift them up to wash off as much blood as I can. I turn off the

147

water, I reach out of the tub for the trash bag and I place the plastic and the clothes inside.

I get out of the tub and I tie the bag up and walk it to the side door of my house and set it just outside of the door.

I walk back to the bathroom and turn the shower on. I stepped into the shower and the scalding hot water didn't seem to bother me. I need the burn of the water to help scrub away the filth of that man's blood. I grab the bar of soap and I scrub and scrub until my hands start to cramp.

I don't feel the need to do it because I want to hide the evidence, I just need the disgusting pig's blood washed away from my body.

I finish in the shower and I go into my bedroom to get dressed. I close my bedroom door and I look at myself in the full length body mirror hanging on the back of my door.

I didn't look physically different but I felt different. I felt evolved, I felt elevated, I felt powerful and for the first time in a long time I felt like I was in charge.

I put on a pair of gym shorts and a white undershirt and I walked back out to the living room. I take a seat at the dining room table and I try to mentally prepare myself for what I am about to see.

The man's computer doesn't have a password to access it, that's sort of curious, maybe it was actually more idiotic on his part but I don't really give it too much thought. He

probably was so egotistical he never even imagined the day where someone would catch onto his sick game.
That man didn't seem like he took his computer anywhere and there definitely weren't any friends or family coming over to his house. Maybe a password wasn't exactly a necessity in his life of revolting immorality.

I begin by searching through the man's images, just like I thought I would find. Folders upon folders of pornography. Sorted by age, gender and physical characteristics. The man didn't have a preference, he didn't discriminate on who he would exploit for his own sexual gratification. But there definitely seemed to be a preferred theme here, children.

I select all of the picture files and move them to the trash can. Are you sure you want to permanently delete the files?

Absolutely.

The video folder is more of the same. It's almost an exact mirroring of the pictures folder as far as categorizing. It made me sick and simultaneously broke my heart just to see the thumbnails. Thinking about these poor children being taken from their parents and their families and forced into this life of abuse. I select all of the videos and move them to the trash can as well. Are you sure you want to permanently delete the files?

For the love of god yes, please erase them now and for forever. Do not ever let anyone lay eyes on these pictures and videos ever again.

Every video file is deleted except for one.

I open the video file and it is a group of people dressed in some kind of black cloaks sitting around a fire. The cloaks all have that same weird symbol stitched on them. They are circling around the fire pit and they are chanting "Azoth, for Azoth" and the circle opens up and there is a little boy standing over a young woman.

The woman is lying unconscious on top of a table. I looked closer, she was tied to some type of symbol, it looks like a medieval symbol or a cross or something similar.

The boy reaches into his cloak and he pulls a dagger out and drives it into the heart of the girl. Blood begins pouring out of her body but she doesn't move, she doesn't wince, she doesn't scream, nothing.

From behind the camera I hear a woman's voice say "now slit her throat Blaine."

The little boy looks over at the camera and nods at the woman standing behind the camera as he slides the dagger into her neck and swipes across her throat. She immediately begins to gurgle and spit up blood.

"Good boy Blaine , you did good." The woman says as she walks from behind the camera and hugs him . All you can see is the symbol on the back of the woman's cloak as she approaches the boy and the cloak engulfs the boy's body as the woman embraces him.

I can't stomach looking through anymore of the computer files under those circumstances so I grab an external hard drive and copy the entire computer contents onto the hard drive. I know that I need to get the computer back to the man's house before anyone else goes by. But it is late and they can wait until the next morning.

I went to bed that night and I slept what might have been the most peaceful night of sleep in my entire life. The next morning I slept through my alarm and when I woke up I called into work and told them that I was not feeling well. That's why I stormed out of the presentation and I must have eaten something tainted.

I drive back to the man's house and park a few doors down. I enter the house through the back door and the kitchen looks the same. I go down into the basement and the man's body is gone. The area where the man was lying has been completely cleaned up.

The washer and dryer are gone, the steel chairs are all gone, all of the laundry is gone. I walk around the basement and it is completely empty. All of the contents of the house have been removed and everything has been cleaned.

I go upstairs and the living room is empty. The bathroom is empty and the bedroom with the desk is completely empty.

"How the hell could someone have cleaned out the entire house, removed a body and cleaned everything in the few hours that I was gone?"

I exit the house through the front door and take the computer back to my car.

I throw the computer in the trunk and drive home.

"What the hell am I going to do with the computer?" I wonder to myself.

I stop on a bridge section of Lake Cook Road and hurl the modem into the Des Plaines River.

"That takes care of that" I tell myself.

I am feeling relieved now that the modem is out of my possession but I can't wrap my mind around the fact that the house was completely cleared out since last night. It wasn't until that moment that I truly knew that the cult that I was now dealing with was serious and that they were capable of almost anything.

Maybe even more so of importance, I knew that the man I killed was not the person in charge of all of this and that I was not in the clear.

Chapter Fourteen

The waiter approaches the table and he has someone trailing behind him carrying two plates with them. The first plate is set down in front of Megan and a plate with the exact same items is set down in front of Blaine.

"Duck a l'orange with a side of black truffle risotto"

"This looks amazing," Megan tells the waiter.

"And we have picked a very special wine to pair with the dish as well. Shiraz from the Rhone Valley region of France. It is a fruity full bodied red wine that can stand on its own when pairing with the strong sauce of the duck. Many like to pair a light white with this type of dish but we prefer to go bold. We also have a Bordeaux we can bring you if you'd like to try that as well."

The waiter fills both glasses and places the bottle in a chiller in the middle of the table.

"Why not, we'll try both, we're here to celebrate tonight."

"As you wish sir, enjoy your meal and I shall return shortly with your Bordeaux as well"

"Judging by what you've told me so far I'm probably going to need two bottles of wine, aren't I?" Megan asks Blaine.

Blaine raises his glass to Megan "to us" he says and takes a large sip from his glass as he continues to speak.

When I arrived home I saw a manila envelope waiting on my porch with that large symbol again drawn in what looked like blood. I knew who it was from there, there was no denying it at this point. I walk slowly up the stairs of the porch battling internally between anticipation and dread of finding out what it could possibly be.

I open the door to my house and bring the package inside. I quickly close the door behind me so nobody walking or driving by can catch a glimpse just in case it's a severed hand or an ear or something from the man's body.

I opened up the package I looked inside and it is a blank dvd. Also inside of the envelope is a note that reads "play me." I immediately walk over to my TV and insert the DVD into the DVD player. I sit down on my couch and press play.

It is a widescreen shot of the man's basement. You see the man walking across the screen towards the stairs and then going up them. Almost immediately you see the man falling down the stairs and hitting his head on the wall. Then I see myself coming down the stairs.

Having to watch and relive everything that followed brings me to a complete meltdown.

"How the hell did they record all of that?" I ask myself.

I see myself kidnapping and torturing the man then killing him. I see myself walking out of the house with the man's computer.

Everything was recorded and they have it all. At the end of
the tape a message scrolls across the screen. "You will
cooperate or we will turn this tape over to the police."

My brain and body begins to shut down at the
overwhelming amount of anxiety and uneasiness from all
of the events of the last several hours.

All I can think to do is lay down on the couch and go to
sleep. I set the alarm on my phone for 5 PM and I crashed
out immediately. I am awoken shortly after by the sound of
someone knocking on my door.

I spring up off of the couch and run to my bedroom to grab
a baseball bat. I look out of all of my windows to see if
anyone is surrounding my house. I open the front door and
there are two police officers standing on my porch in
uniform. "I'm sorry sir were you busy" the officers asked
me.

"I was just sleeping on my couch, I've had a long last
couple days. I haven't been able to sleep much at night." I
responded.

"That's why we're here sir" the cops respond.

My heart drops into my stomach as I prepare to be arrested
for murder.

"We received a few calls about people wandering through
backyards recently. Have you seen anything? We've just
been canvassing the neighborhood because of continuous

complaints. Your neighbor said they may have seen someone in your yard last night"

"In my yard last night? Not that I saw. I had a pizza delivered the other night but that was nothing out of the ordinary. Last night I crashed out kind of early because I had a work presentation I had been working on for months."

"I thought you said you weren't sleeping at night lately?" the officers ask.

"Well prior to last night I had not been."

"I see. Well if you remember anything or if you see anything new here is my card, feel free to give me a call."

"No problem officer. By the way my parents are cops around here, maybe you know them."

I tell them about Mother and Father and how they have been retired for several years now. They were partners but they got shot and had to leave the force. My parents used to love telling me that story when I was a child.

"What did you say their names were again?" the cop asked.

"Carrie and Brent Acadia" I responded.

The first cop turns to his partner and asks him "Aren't those cops who came up missing after their little boy was abducted like twenty years ago?" His partner responds "That's a really fucked up joke."

"I would never joke about something like that. I'm...I 'm sorry but you must have the names mixed up" I tell them unsure of what they are talking about.

"There was a manhunt for several weeks looking for that little boy. Then in the thick of it both officers went missing. You should look it up, I might be mistaken on the names I suppose. You have a good day sir."

I shut the door and grab my car keys off of the dining room table.

"I need to get the hell out of the house for a little while," I tell myself.

I drove over to My parents house, out of everyone they would be the only people I could really trust. I knock on the living room door. I get no answer. I knock louder. Still no answer.

I still have a key to my parents house so I use the key and enter through the front door.

I walk through the door and Mother comes rushing to meet me at the door. She comes to the front door wearing just a robe and her hair is disheveled. She seems sort of embarrassed and she's out of breath. She definitely wasn't just sitting around watching tv.

"Oh hi honey, this is some really bad timing" Mother tells me.

"I don't care if you and Father are having sex I just need somewhere I can relax for a little while and clear my head" I tell Mother as I storm past her.

She tries to stop me from entering but I easily pass by her.

Once I stepped inside I couldn't believe what I saw.

There are piles of clothes everywhere, there are piles of people everywhere. They are kissing, they are groping, they are moaning, they are having sex on nearly every available surface and in every available room in the house.

I look back at Mother in surprise and disgust.

"I tried to stop you, " she told him.

"What the hell Mom!?" I exclaim.

"Give me five minutes and I'll meet you in your car and explain."

I ran out of the house back to my car and waited until I saw mother come walking out of the house in the same robe but now she was wearing sweatpants and a shirt.

"At least she put some clothes on," I tell myself.

She gets in the front passenger seat next to me. "Where do you want me to start?" she asks him.

"I don't know Mom, how about the giant orgy in your house. There were people literally fucking everywhere in there, on everything. In my childhood home Mom, what the hell? What the hell is going on Mom?."

"Your Father and I are swingers Blaine, we have been pretty much all of your life. Since you grew up and moved out of the house we've just been able to be more open about it." Mother explains to me.

"And you just have orgies at your house regularly? Have you been having orgies in the house the whole time? Like then I was a little kid and I fell asleep people were just fucking outside of my bedroom door?"

"No, no, no, this is the first time. Since we were moving we thought it would be our last chance to host a party of our own. We've been going to everyone else's parties for most of our lives and we wanted to show some hospitality."

"Some hospitality? I get opening up your home for some drinks and what not but opening up your entire body to the neighborhood to come and"

Mother cuts me off "to come eat a slice of pie or a mouthful of cake?" she says as she laughs.

"Gross mother."

I am amazed at how openly my Mother can just tell me all of this information. She isn't batting an eye, there isn't the tiniest bit of insecurity in her voice. This woman really enjoys this.

I am disgusted, not because of the sex or the idea of the orgy in general but because Mother is the center of all of it, and she loves being in that position. Not that she is unattractive or revolting or anything but it is just hard to picture your mother being the center of attention for all of these men and women to lust for.

"My life is falling apart Mother and I finally come to you and Father for some comfort and understanding and I'm greeted with a gangbang on the dining room table where I ate all I meals as a child"

Mother laughs "you should have called me first before you decided to stop by ."

"I just really need somewhere to stay away from my house for a few days, Mom. I have a lot going on right now. I can't exactly explain it. Can I just wait out here until you guys are done? I just really need to be here right now." I asked Mom.

"Absolutely honey. It might be a little while longer, you can't rush these things but I will let you know then it's safe to enter. Unless you want to come in Blaine. I will make sure your Father and I stay away from whatever room you try to occupy. It might be good for you to let out a little tension."

"You can't be a serious Mom."

"Why not?"

"Well I guess my first reservation would be that I'm not comfortable having sex with women that you and Father both just had sex with. Secondly, every person in there is like sixty, no offense or anything, but no thanks."

"Well, not all of them are that old. Believe it or not, there are some men and women in there around your age, but I get it."

She tries to kiss me on the cheek before she gets out of the car.

I started to pull away "Mom, you probably just had twenty different dicks in your mouth, please don't try and kiss me, that's just really gross."

"Twenty is a bit of an exaggeration. There's maybe only nine men in there, besides I usually go after the women in these parties, she tells me.

I am unable to get a response out before Mother gets out of the car and hurries back into the house.

I am starting to realize that I really don't know much about my parents. I spent my whole life living with them but I never really made an attempt to get to know them. I'm always preoccupied with other things.

Apparently I was too busy trying to exploit children, murdering young women in ritual sacrifices and being recruited into joining a cult as a kid. I never really took the time to understand that my parents were probably the most sexually enlightened people I've ever met.

I wait in my car for another two hours until I see everyone finally start to spill out of the house.

"Orgies really take that long to finish? I couldn't imagine doing anything for that long let alone having sex and not just regular sex, sex with multiple people. Trying to give multiple people blowjobs or hand jobs or going down on multiple women for several hours just seems like work. That isn't even mentioning the fact that there is absolutely no way in hell that I could even stay wet or stimulated that long, what about you? Are you interested in trying that? " Megan asks Blaine.

"Umm, I, uhh that is not really the response that I was prepared to get after that part of the story but no I don't think I would be into anything like that."

Chapter Fifteen

The waiter returns to the table with the bottle of Bordeaux that he just promised he would be returning with soon. He sets it in the middle of the table into a new wine chiller next to the previous bottle of wine.

"Is there anything else I can bring you at this time?" The waiter asks them.

"No, we should be fine, thank you very much," Blaine says trying to hurry the waiter off.

Megan starts laughing "looks like you are going to need that whole bottle to yourself after having to relive that, not me. Go on with your story about your sex crazed orgy loving parents."

Once everyone leaves the house I finally build up the courage to get out of the car and walk to the front door and knock. I learned my lesson a few hours ago, the last time I tried to come into the house unannounced. Mother answers the door, fully clothed this time.

"Come on in smartass" she says to me.

I follow her in through the door and Father is standing there at the door with my arms open to give me a hug. I am a little hesitant and look Father up and down inspecting him for any signs of nudity or randomly discarded piles of bodily fluids that may have stained his clothing and could easily brush up against me.

"Good to see you buddy," Father tells me.

"Mother told you I walked in on the orgy didn't she?" I ask him sheepishly.

"She sure did Blaine" Father replies trying his best to hold back his laughter

"Well Father, did she also tell you that she invited me to join in on your little senior orgy?"

Father looks over at Mother and raises his eyebrows and gives her a look of uncertainty "no, no she did not, I guess she just decided to exclude that part of the story when she decided to fill me in."

"I told him that he could pick a girl or two and go off into a room by themselves and we wouldn't interrupt them so that it wouldn't be weird for him" Mother begins to explain herself.

"I'm not sure that is any better, sweetheart," Father says to Mother.

I try to change the conversation to something a little more paced.
"So is there anywhere in this immediate area that is safe for me to sit and to relax for a little while? You know somewhere that someone hasn't just ejaculated all over?" I ask Mother and Father sarcastically.

Father points to the dining room table and looks over at Mother, she shakes her head no back at him. I try again pointing into the living room at a reclining chair. This time her eyes open big as she shakes her head no in an even more visible way.

It must be her favorite spot or something.

I looked into the living room where Father pointed and looked back at Mother as she shook her head at him. I think back to what Mother said earlier about preferring women when they attend these parties and vivid recreations of three women taking turns chowing down on her as she sits spread eagle on the chair floods my mind.

"What the hell is wrong with me?" I think to myself.

"Dear god can I just sit on the couch and watch some TV for a little while then, I'll just lay a blanket down or something" I say laughing.

"It's not like everyone walks around squirting and spraying fluids everywhere Blaine, do we need to have the talk again about how sex works?" Mother asks me.

"Please save me the details Mother I just saw all the way the inside of a woman's uterus and anus from four feet away, as four men took turns putting their fists inside of her, I think I have a pretty clear understanding now if I didn't before"

I walk into the living room and plop down on the couch and turn on the TV. "Do you want me to make you anything to eat, are you thirsty?" Mother asks. Very typical of a mother to offer food and drink even in such awkward circumstances.

"I'm starving, I'm thirsty, I'm tired, I'm exhausted ...I really just needed to be at home with you guys. Some places just feel more comfortable and safe and right now more than anything I need to be where I can just feel like myself and feel secure." I tell Mother and Father.

"Is there anything you want to get off your chest buddy?" Father asks me.

"I really don't want to talk about it right now. Can we all just sit here and watch TV together and have a sandwich or something?" I ask them.

Mother walks over and starts to rub my back a little bit and kisses me on the forehead. "No problem honey, let me make you something to eat, your Father and I could probably go for some food too." Mother heads into the kitchen.

Father walks over and sits down next to me.

"If you are in any kind of trouble you can tell us, you know that right? If anyone in the world would understand it, we would understand, we've been through and seen everything Blaine " Father tells me.

"Yeah I know, when I get a little piece of mind back I will let you guys know."

"So buddy did that old computer of yours boot up and work or was it just trash?" Father asks me.

"No, it was just trash. I'm not sure what was wrong with it. I plugged the thing in and it started making all kinds of weird noises. The screen started flashing all kinds of different colors and then it went black. I tried turning it off and on a few times before it started to smoke so I just threw it in the trash. I'm not so sure I really want to know what was on there anyway, I started thinking about it and maybe it was for the best I just forgot about all of that."

"Well it was out in that garage for a long time, maybe it got some kind of water damage, or maybe the bugs or mice got into it. That really is a shame buddy, you looked pretty excited about it."

I couldn't even begin to comprehend how I would work up the courage to begin explaining to my parents all of the things that I've been through in the last few days.

Where would I start if I decided to open up? From the sick fat pedophile Don stalking me and breaking into my house on more than one occasion. Being followed from my house to work. Being followed from the parking structure to where I work. Having to deal with the paranoia of being tracked and followed everywhere that I wanted to go.

Completely shitting the bed on the presentation in front of
the man who has been stalking me and probably losing my
job because of it. Having to murder the man who has been
stalking him. Being questioned by the police. Going back
to the man's house who I killed and finding it completely
cleaned out.

A video tape of me killing the man being sent to my house.
A video tape of me as a child killing some innocent
woman. Having to dispose of murder weapons and criminal
evidence. Then to top it off I almost witnessed my own
Mother getting gangbanged on top of the couch I was now
laying on.

I decided to hold off on opening up to my parents for now,
I've had a lot on my mind and I really just need to reboot.

"Do you mind if I just lay down and close my eyes for a
little bit?" I ask Father .

"Not at all, I 'll grab you a pillow and a blanket" Father
tells him.

"One more thing Father, did you change the Wi-Fi
password?" I asked.

"Nope bud, it's still the same."

I close my eyes and I start to doze off.

*Father heads into a spare bedroom down the hallway and
returns with a blanket and pillow. By the time Father gets
back to the living room Blaine is already asleep. Father*

throws the blanket over top of Blaine and sets the pillow on the back of the couch.

Father walks into the kitchen and walks up to Mom. Father stands behind her and he grabs her by the waist and kisses her on her ear. "I can't believe Blaine really walked in on all of that today, that's gonna stick with him for a while," Father tells her.

"We're just lucky he didn't come over last week then we had that younger teenage girl over for that sacrifice, that may have made him a little queasy" Mother says.

"You never know he might have liked it, he is unpredictable," Father says.

"You're right about that, I used to love being a part of those parties when I was a kid." Mother tells him, she goes on "Remember when Blaine was willing to stab his own birth Mother for us? Do you ever think he will come around again?" Mother asks.

"I'm sure he will, we've been doing our best to get him back. I mean he killed Don earlier so he's definitely headed down the right path" Father says.

"Yeah, he looked like he liked doing it too," Mother says.

"It shouldn't take much more of you messaging him to get Blaine back on our side. Remember how easy it was to convince him when he was a kid?" Father says, "You

really know what to say and how to get in his head sweetheart."

"Oh I remember, Blaine just wants what he has always wanted... to be loved and accepted. His parents couldn't give him that. That's why they lost that poor boy, but we found him and we saved him. That's why they had to die. Letting a great boy like that just slip through their fingers" Mother says.

"Do you remember when we first got Blaine? He was so quiet and sheltered, he was like a little shelter dog. The only thing that could open him up was that damn computer. Your suggestion of giving it back to him was a great idea" Father tells Mom.

"I can't believe he fell for the whole come over and helped us clean out the garage trick." Mother says.

"Blaine's a good kid, you know he wants to help, he would do anything for you," Father says.

"So when do you think we should break it to him?" Mother asks.

"He hasn't wanted to talk about all of it just yet. Just let him soak on it for a little while, Blaine will come around" Father tells her.

They both walk back out into the living room where Blaine is sleeping.

Mother bends over and gives him a kiss on the forehead while Father pats his shoulder.

"Blaine sure is a great kid though, He's grown up to be such a responsible adult." Mother says.

Mother and Father look at each other and nod.

Chapter Sixteen

"This duck is absolutely amazing Blaine, I don't think that I've ever tried anything like it."

"Yeah, it is."

"What's wrong? You don't like it?"

"No, no, nothing like that it's just having to relive all of this sucks. It makes me wonder about some of the things I might have missed that could have clued me in sooner."

"What do you mean by that?"

Blaine continues on.

I wake up on the couch of my parents living room and I smell something good coming from the kitchen. I get up off the couch and see my parents sitting at the dining room table.

"Good morning buddy we've been waiting for you to wake up?" Father says,

"Morning? How long did I sleep for?" I asked.

"About two hours, dinners ready if you're hungry" Father tells me.

"Take a seat honey, I'll make you a plate" Mother says.

I take a seat at the table, my stomach starts growling, I can't remember the last time I actually had a home cooked meal.

Mother walks back to the table with a plate in hand.

"I made your favorite food for you, meat loaf, mashed potatoes and gravy."

"Fuck yes!" I exclaimed as I can't wait to eat.

"Language at the table young man" Mother tells me.

"Sorry Mom, I'm just really excited I haven't had this in so long" I said as I started shoveling food into my face.

My parents are asking a million questions as I am eating:

"Have you met any nice girls?"
"How is work going?"
"Do you have any new career goals?"
"Are you seeing anyone? More than one person?"
"Are you gay? You know you can tell us."

If you let me finish eating I promise I will answer all of your questions. They stared intently at me waiting for me to polish off my plate so that they could continue with the interrogation. They were taking a genuine interest in me and for the first time I was open to actually sharing what was going on in my life.

I finished my plate and I put it in the sink and rinsed it off.

"So what have you guys packed so far for the move?" I asked.

"Just little things. Some clothes, some extra linens, towels, small things like that" Mother tells me.

"Do you have any photo albums or anything packed up? I'd really like to look through some old pictures. I guess going through the garage and finding an old computer just made me miss my childhood" I tell them. "Do you remember what I was like as a kid? Was I really mean or vindictive?"

"Heavens no Blaine. You were quiet, you were reserved, you weren't very social. But mean or vindictive? Absolutely not. Sit right here and I'll go grab some pictures for you" Mother gets up and walks out to the garage.

She comes back into the house with a big plastic tub.

She sets it in front of me and I open the tub. The first thing I take out is a diploma and a cap and gown. There is a note from what looks like my old teachers and principal praising my academia but it looks like it's in Mother and Father's handwriting.

"See I can't even remember my own graduation really" I say.

"You were homeschooled, we bought you those things so you could take those studio graduation pictures, we wanted you to feel normal," Father tells me.

"I was homeschooled? Why?" I ask them.

"Because you hated school. We tried to put you in school and you just shut down. You wouldn't come out of your room for a week after that. All you did was hide and cry, you ate a peanut butter sandwich four times a day for a week. That's all you would touch so we decided to homeschool you" Mother explains to me.

I dig through more pictures of me and my parents at their house at birthday parties with a bunch of strangers I don't recognize. I see pictures of them hiking through the woods, of them at the carnival of them in swimming pools.

But one thing immediately stands out to me .

"Almost all of these pictures are from the same time frame. I was like eleven or twelve in almost all of these pictures" I say to them with an inquisitive tone.

"Yes, Blaine, what are you trying to get at?" Father asks me.

"Where are the pictures from when I was a baby?" I asked.

"What do you mean Blaine? Why would we have pictures of you as a baby? Mother asks me.

"Well I would assume it's normal for parents to have pictures of their child as a baby, am I wrong?" I asked them.

"We didn't adopt you until you were ten years old, Blaine. You don't remember being adopted?" Mother asks me really softly and compassionately.

"I was adopted? Well what happened to my parents? Why did they put me up for adoption?" I asked them.

"We're not sure, we were told that your parents just let you go one day and they took off. You were left stranded on the side of the road. We were told that your parents were addicts, it was tossed out around the station that you might have been sold off for drug money. So we heard about the case at work and we took you in." Father begins explaining to me.

"Well, can I see the adoption paperwork or something at least?" I asked.

"It was never really official Blaine. We didn't want the story to make it to the news and we definitely didn't want you to get put into foster care. Your Father and I had dealt with child services before and we knew how the system worked, foster care or a home was the absolute worst place you could have gone" Mother explains to me.

"I'm sorry I 'm just having a hard time comprehending all of this. I was adopted by you guys. No, I was found by you guys and taken in because my drug addict parents sold me off for crack money? Rather than adopting me the right way with paperwork you just moved me into your house? Then you homeschooled me because I was too mentally fucked up to go to school?"

I began to get really loud and angry "Do I have that right? Is all of that right. I'M A FUCKING CRACK BABY ORPHAN WHO WAS TAKEN IN BY TWO EX COPS BECAUSE I WAS SOLD FOR FUCKING CRACK MONEY TO TWEAKER PARENTS? IS THAT RIGHT!?"

I get up and I storm up the stairs into my old bedroom and I slam the door behind me. I bury my head into my pillow and I start crying, I just feel overwhelmed and broken down.

"Call them now. Get them over here, we have to start convincing Blaine now" Mother tells Father.

Father picks up the phone and makes a call to two men.

I am in my room playing the events of the day over in my brain. I starts thinking about how my parents left me, how my new parents are crazy sex fiends and how the house I grew up in is getting sold.

How everything I thought I knew about my life has completely been flipped upside down all because of a fucking computer.

The same computer that saved my life as a kid is the very thing that is ruining my life as an adult ... oh the irony.

I hear knocking on my door.

"Go away!" I scream at the door.

"Blaine, there are some detectives here to talk to you," Father tells me through the door.

"There are detectives here? At my parents house? They want to see me? How much worse can this fucking day get?" I wonder to myself.

I walk downstairs and outside where there are two detectives waiting for me. They are both in blue suits and wearing sunglasses.

One of them was average height I would say probably around 5'9" 190 lbs or so, he had blonde hair and brown eyes. The other one was very tall, probably 6' 7". He wasn't very muscular, maybe 210 lbs., I remember thinking he didn't exactly fit the profile of most cops I had seen. He had dark black hair and brown eyes as well.

These weren't your dumb average patrol cops like the ones who visited me at my house. These are either real detectives who know what the fuck they are doing or these are members of that sadistic pedophile cult. Either way they tracked me to my parents house and now I put my parents life at risk.

"Sir, can you come with us for questioning?" the detectives ask me.

I follow them to a police car and get in the back.

I see the detectives walk back over to my parents. Their backs are to me so I can't make out exactly what they are saying.

"Hopefully you two can straighten him out a little bit and make him remember where he came from" Father tells them.

"Yes sir, we will do our best," the detectives tell Father .

"Doing your best is not good enough. If Blaine does not come back completely convinced that joining the Order of Azoth is the best thing for him then you two will be dead next" Mother tells them.

She begins crying and covering her face, she needs to paint a picture of pain and anguish for Blaine to see. She needs to lull him into a false sense of debt to her.

The tall one gets in the driver's seat and the blonde one gets in the passenger seat.

The car pulls off and I see Father wrap his arm around Mother trying to console her as she cries.

Chapter Seventeen

"The two detectives found you at your parents house and they took you away for questioning? Did they show you a warrant or anything?" Megan asks Blaine intently.

"I guess I didn't really think to ask them. I just wanted to get them away from my parents" Blaine explains to Megan "I was more concerned with keeping my parents safe at that point and that's all I had going through my mind. I was going to make these guys pay for coming there."

"And you were completely sure that they were not actual police officers."

"Absolutely not. I had a hunch that they weren't but in no way was I completely sure. My gut was all I had up to that point and everything I was starting to piece together seemed to be right on point so far."

They drove me to an office building a few blocks away.

They get out of the car and the tall one opens the car door for me "Follow us Blaine."

I get out of the car and I follow them to the front of the building. I watch the blonde guy enter some key code that I can't make out and he opens up the door.

"Follow us sir" the blonde one instructs me.

I follow them inside of the building. All of the windows are blacked out so you can't see what is going on inside. There is a desk with a few chairs on each side of the table. In the corner there is a mini fridge, a coffee pot and a microwave on top of a folding table.

I dropped my head in disappointment, and I accepted my fate now "If you guys are going to kill me just go ahead. I'm not joining your cult of homicidal fucking pedophiles" I tell them in defeat.

"Sir, we are FBI agents. We assure you that we are not here to kill you. They found the body of a man named Donald Mabury dismembered and tied up in a couple garbage bags thrown into some brush by your house" they explained to me.

"Donald Mabury, that name sounds familiar but I'm not sure I know him." I tell the officers as flashbacks of me taping the man to a chair, choking him out then beating the man with a steel chair come flashing to mind.

"He was a big shot in the company that you work for, did you know that?" they ask me.

"Was he a fat guy with a ponytail?" I ask them.

"Yes, that's him" they tell me.

"Yeah I met him for the first time yesterday at work. What does him dying have to do with me? Am I a suspect or something?" I asked.

"No, no nothing like that, not in his murder. However, you were caught up in a case I was involved in several years ago and we wanted to see what you could remember" the detectives explained to me.

"What kind of case?" I ask?

"We broke up a pedophile network a few years ago. Your computer was confiscated in the process. We found out through detective work that you were being targeted by this man Donald Maybury specifically to help get material for trading. I guess when you got older he found a way to get you into his company to keep you close and keep tabs on you. You were taken away from your parents for several months and you were put into a juvenile detention facility. The judges were wanting to try you as an adult but your parents fought for you. They convinced the judge that due to your tough upbringing you were susceptible to manipulation and you couldn't be held accountable for everything you did."

"And Donald Mabury was in charge of everything?" I asked them.

"As far as we know, yes. Unless there's any new information that you feel would be useful to us" the detectives tell me hoping to get any new information out of me.

"No, nothing that I can think of," I told them.

"Well then we'll take you back to your parents. Your parents who protected you from that man and ensured that you didn't spend the majority of your adult life in prison. Sounds like pretty great parents to me. Regardless of how they were able to take you in, the tall detective looks over at the blonde one and hits him in the chest. He does so in a way to suggest that maybe he said something he shouldn't have.

"Do you guys know my parents or something?" I asked.

"Well we uh we talked to them a little bit before they went to grab you from upstairs at the house" the detectives explained to me.

That seems like a fairly logical reasoning at that point in time and I know that my parents are the only ones that I can trust.

"Well then if that's it let us take you back to your parents" the tall detective says to me.

"Do you have a bathroom here?' I ask them.

I went into the bathroom and I stared at myself in the mirror. I know who these men are, they are not FBI agents, they work for that cult. There isn't a doubt in my mind and I knew what I had to do now.

I walk back out into the area where the desk is.

"Alright, I'm ready" I tell them.

The two men start to walk out of the building in front of me leading the way just like they did on our way in.

I immediately pull the weapon of the blonde man in the back out from his holster. I put the gun to the back of the man's head and I pulled the trigger. Immediately blood and brain matter spray from the hole in the man's previously intact skull all over my face and clothes. I wipe the blood from my eyes and I point the gun at the tall man.

"You get in here now or you will end up like your friend here" I direct the tall man as I motion to the blonde man lying lifeless on the floor.

The tall man walks back inside of the building. "You don't want to do this , think of your parents" he says to me.

"My parents are the reason I have to do this. I've put them at risk, you coming to their house has put them at risk. I know all of you are following me and I lead you right to my parents. Now I have to protect them" I tell the man. "Now get down on your knees."

The tall man stares blankly at me. I lower the weapon and fire a shot into the man's knee cap. The blast drops the man to his knees and now he is on my level.

"From this point on you will do exactly what I say, do I make myself clear?" I walk behind the tall man and put the muzzle of the weapon to the back of the man's head between the bottom of his skull and the top of his neck.

"Now you will tell me everything that you know about the fucking cult that keeps following me" I demand the tall man.

"I have no idea what you are talking about," the tall man says to me.

I take the butt of the gun and strike the tall man in the back of the head. He falls forward onto his stomach and I sit on his back pressing the muzzle of the gun into the back of his head again.

"I will give you one more chance, tell me what you know" I shout at him as I slide my finger onto the trigger.

"I'm not telling you shit. If this is what it takes to make you realize your potential then do it. Pull that trigger, I will die a martyr, your parents will love me" the detective tells me with his face buried into the cold concrete floor.

I pull the trigger and I can see the blood soaked concrete floor peaking through from the hole that has been put into the tall man's head.

Chapter Eighteen

The waiter approaches the table and sees that the food has been cleared from both plates.

"May I take your plates from you?" he asks.

Megan can't bring herself to find any words to respond.

"Yes, we're done, thank you" Blaine responds to the waiter.

"Is there anything else I can bring you at this time?" the waiter asks them.

"Umm we should be fine with our wine and everything for now."

"I will have dessert for you soon then." The waiter walks to the kitchen area again.

Megan is still speechless.

I make a sweep around the building to see if there's anything I can use to help get rid of these two bodies, if not get rid of them at least to move them for now. I found a few rolls of duct tape in a storage room along with a couple rolls of old carpet.

They must have torn the carpet up in favor of these grey concrete floors, I imagine the blood is easier to clean off of concrete than carpet for them.

I lay the blonde man in the middle of a roll of carpet and fold the ends around him. I drag the body and the body starts to slide out as the carpet begins to unfold.

"This is not going to work."

I lay the body on the end of the carpet and I try rolling it again. This time I'm able to get a good roll to completely secure the body in the carpet. I used duct tape and wrapped it around the rolls several times to make sure it wouldn't unravel when I started dragging it out.

I go out to the men's car and I open up the trunk of the car.

Inside of the trunk I see four large black trash bags. I open the bags and inside of the bags I see a bunch of different clothes. Uniforms, nursing scrubs, business suits, they look like an assortment of costumes. These men must have been following me the last few days, they have every type of outfit you can think of.

I take two of the trash bags out of the trunk and I close the trunk as I walk back inside. I go over to the body that's rolled up in the carpet and I unravel it. I strip all of the clothes off of the blonde man and throw my bloody suit into a pile. I walked over to the other body of the tall man and I stripped all of his clothes off as well. I took all of the clothes and threw them into the pile of clothes from the blonde man's body.

I dumped the trash bags full of new clothes onto the table and I sorted through them. I believe if I put a different set of clothes on them it will be harder for the police to identify the bodies if they are found.

The first outfit that grabs my attention is a pair of gray coveralls. I take the coveralls over to the blonde man and I put the outfit on him. He looks like a mechanic or a shop person, something along those lines, that's believable.

The second body of the tall man I dress in a pair of jeans and a flannel shirt. Just a normal tall person walking down the street who got abducted and got his head blown off, then his body was wrapped in carpet and dumped somewhere. That will draw a lot less attention than a guy dressed in a suit with a fake badge on him.

I drag the first body of the blonde man back onto the carpet and roll him up again. I tape the rolls of carpet and drag him outside to the trunk of the car. I have a little bit of a hard time lifting the body up and throwing it into the trunk.

I walked back to the second body, I wrapped him up like the first guy. I tape up the roll of carpet and I drag it out to the trunk. The body is probably 20 lbs. heavier than the first one so it takes even more effort to get him into the trunk.

I walk back inside of the building and take a look around. I see pools of blood on the concrete and drag marks going out to the parking lot where the car was.

"Who gives a shit" I told myself as I got in the car and drove off.

I spent the next two hours scouting out locations that would be perfect for dumping off two full grown men rolled in old shitty carpet secured with duct tape. Where exactly would something like that look fairly natural?

I drove to the overpass where I dumped off the computer modem previously.

"No there is way too many people around" I tell myself

I drive around to all of the parks I know of within five miles and every single one of them are full of people. This isn't something that I have ever had to put an extended amount of thought into.

I get out my phone and I type "where are most abandoned bodies found" into the search bar. Before I press the search I get a feeling that my phone might be bugged or tracked or something by the FBI or someone. This is all very new to me and I am getting used to the idea of constantly being under surveillance. It takes a little bit of time to completely reprogram your brain into not automatically pulling out your phone for advice.

I erase it, put my phone away and I keep driving.

I find myself going back to my house. I pulled into my driveway and I sat there for a few minutes trying to gather my thoughts and reflect on the current situation. I turned the car off and I walked up my porch and I opened the door to my house.

Once I enter the house I see that the TV is on. The TV is playing a recording and I sat down on the couch and began watching it.

It's video footage of the building those two fake detectives took me to. I watch as I am questioned, then as I walk into the bathroom. I see myself walk out of the bathroom, I watch as I kill both of those men. I see myself roll the bodies and take them outside. I see myself walk back in, look around then leave.

I turn to my old computer that has been sitting on the coffee table ever since I stormed out earlier. The desktop is still pulled up. I logged onto instant messenger.

SoccerDude2k1 is online.

He sends me a message.

xXBlaineDamage88Xx: The body count is up to three on your end now. How much longer do you want to keep going?
SoccerDude2k1: I have more people that are willing to die for our cause than people you are capable of killing.
xXBlaineDamage88Xx: We'll see about that. You brought my parents into this. You put their lives at risk and I will stop for nothing and no one to make sure you never have an opportunity to harm them.

I received a picture message.

It is a picture of my parents' house.

SoccerDude2k1: Do you want me to keep going?
xXBlaineDamage88Xx: Fuck you, I will find you and I will
kill you like those other three.

I received another picture message.

It's a picture of my parents' living room.

SoccerDude2k1: This can all end at any time, Blaine .
xXBlaineDamage88Xx: This will only end when I kill every
single one of you sick fucks.
.

I start to receive picture message after picture message
continuously.

A picture of my Mother naked with a mask covering her
face. A picture of my Father naked with a mask on his
face. A picture of several people dressed in cloaks in My
parents' dining room. I receive pictures of several men and
women surrounding my mother and father and they are tied
down to the dining room table.

xXBlaineDamage88Xx: I WILL FUCKING KILL YOU! I
WILL FIND YOU AND I WILL KILL YOU.
SoccerDude2k1: You have already found us Blaine. All you
have to do is come home. We will be waiting for you . You
should have never left. It is time for you to come home, all
of this can be yours.

I stand up and I storm out of the house. I am heading to my
parents house. I run every light I come to and I drive as fast
as I can until I get there. I pulled up in front of my parents'

house and I got out and I started screaming "I'm here you sick mother fuckers. Come get me, I am here, come do what you need to do!"

The garage door of my parents' house slowly begins to open and I see a silhouette start to come towards me.

Chapter Nineteen

"Megan, will you please say something to me about all of this? You sitting there like that all catatonic like and not saying anything is really starting to make me feel nervous and scared."

Megan stares blankly at Blaine from across the table.

My parents come running out to meet me in the street and calm me down. "What happened to the detectives? Why do you have their car? Well Blaine, what did they want to talk to you about?" Mother and Father take turns asking me.

"Where are they? They sent me pictures of you two, you were tied down to your kitchen table. They were standing around you about to kill you" I alarmingly began explaining to them.

"No one is here buddy, it's just us. Calm down, we're fine. What did the detectives want to walk to you about?" My parents ask me.

"They wanted to know if I had any information on a man who turned up dead today. They said I was part of some kind of FBI sting a few years ago that turned up a bunch of pedophiles and my computer was part of it. They said that you guys were able to get me off with just a few months of time in a juvenile facility" I tell them.

"Why the hell did they have to bring that back up?" Father says to Mother.

"Why didn't you guys ever bring it up to me?" I ask them.

"You were taken from us for almost a year Blaine . While you were there you had gone through serious therapy to help you get rid of all of that guilt. Why would we try and bring that up to you? We know that you are sensitive and that would only send you spiraling again" Mother explains to me.

"I appreciate everything you've done for me, I know I don't say it enough but I do. I am sorry for everything I have put you through" I tell them. "But how did you guys prevent me from going to jail?"

"We just know some powerful people Blaine, when you are involved in the work that we did you find ways to network and create connections with people in high places. Sometimes you find yourself in a position of power without really ever realizing how you got there in the first place" Mother tells me.

I lead both of my parents to the trunk of the car, I open the trunk and inside of it are the bodies of the two detectives wrapped in old carpet and duct tape.

"I hope you both still know some powerful people because I really need to get rid of these guys. They didn't work for the FBI , they were part of some cult that's been following me around for the last few days. I killed a man named Donald Maybury and now I've killed these two. I didn't

194

know what else to do so I came here. These two men followed me to your house and I had to kill them to protect you" I begin to hyperventilate as I am struggling to get out complete sentences. "I'm sorry Mother and Father I won't let anyone hurt you."

Mother grabs me by the hand and they walk me back inside. We all sat at the dining room table. Father gets up and opens the fridge, he grabs out three beers and sets one in front of everyone at the table.

"Father, there are two bodies in a trunk outside of your house, now isn't the time." I told him.

"If there was ever a time for a beer Blaine, trust me, it's now. Don't worry about those bodies, I will take care of it" Mother tells me and she rubs my back to comfort me.

"Where were we before your meltdown earlier? Want to look at more pictures, do you have any more questions you want to ask us?" Father asks me.

"Can you tell me about my parents? Two cops came by my house the other day and I told them my parents used to be cops and I said your names and they told me that there were two cops by your names who had gone missing after their son was abducted or something."

"They said that it was our names that happened to?" Father asks me.

195

"Yeah they said it was Carrie and Brent Acadia" I told them.

My parents look at each other, their faces go blank.

"Well bud that's uh that's because" Father tries to spit out before Mother interrupts "That's because our last name is not Acadia honey. Did you hit your head or something?"

"What do you mean? My name is Blaine Acadia, it always has been." I tell Mother.

"No it's not Blaine, honey look at your drivers license" Mother tells me.

I reach into my back pocket and I pull out my wallet. I removed my drivers license from my wallet and read it out loud to my parents.

"Blaine Tyler Holly"

"Yes Blaine, your last name is Holly. We are Carrie and Brent Holly" Mother tells me.

"Those officers probably did recognize the name Acadia, maybe they were killed I'm not sure. But what I am sure of is that your last name is Holly" Father reassures me.

"Do you guys care if I go sit in my old room for a little while, I feel like I just might need some quiet time to myself?"

I get up from the table and head upstairs. Mother and Father are still sitting at the table talking.

"You know he's going to go upstairs and immediately jump on his phone and start searching for that name right?" Father says to Mother.

"Yes. That's exactly what we want him to do. The faster that he finds out who he thinks he is supposed to be, the faster we can show him who he truly is" Mother says.

Upstairs I shut and lock the door to my old bedroom.

I pulled out my phone and immediately began searching for the names Carrie and Brent Acadia. The search engine pulls up dozens of articles about the couple:

"Slayed Cops Were Husband and Wife."
"Husband and Wife Cop Team Goes Missing."
"Bodies of Missing Cops Still Nowhere To Be Found."

I see one article that catches my eye.

"Carrie and Brent Acadia Go Missing After Search For Son Blaine."

I began to search for Blaine Acadia, and I found several more articles. I click that first article and it says:

"Blaine Acadia was abducted from his home in Joliet, Illinois. He was left at home with a babysitter while his parents, Officers Carrie and Brent Acadia were at work."

I click through several articles looking for pictures. I found one article with pictures of the husband and wife. The father doesn't look familiar but I swore I had seen the Mother's face before somewhere.

I looked through more articles hoping to find a picture of the boy.

The battery power on my phone flashes 1% as I pull up an article that has a picture of the boy my phone dies. I walk back downstairs to where my parents are still sitting at the dining room table.

They curiously look up at me, waiting for me to speak.

Can I use your guys' computer, my phone died?

"Yeah no problem, just don't go searching through everything. There probably are some things on there you don't want to see" Father tells me and winks.

"Great, just what I need to see more pictures of Mom's ass" I say out loud and we all laugh.

I walked to the computer room across the hall from my old bedroom and went to log on.

I see a user profile for Mother which I guess probably has a ton of naked pictures of old women and a profile for Father which probably has an equal amount of naked women but has a higher chance of the pictures containing Mom.

I clicked on the guest. I brought up Google and searched for Blaine Holly. The search engine turns up my Facebook and Linked In profiles.

I searched again for Blaine Acadia. I found an article that contains pictures of the boy. I scroll until I get to a picture. It's the same little boy from the video at the cult gathering where he stabs that woman. That's where I recognize the woman from the video being killed.

That sick fucker Donald abducted that little boy and then forced him to kill his own Mother.

I let the information I just saw sink it and allow myself time to process everything.

"The little boy in that video was me. I was abducted, I killed my mom."

I get up and I quietly close the door to the computer room and I lock it.

I log onto Father's profile.

I began to search through all of his folders, all of the photos and all of the videos.

My parents had to know that I was involved in all of them. That was the reason they were able to prevent me from going to prison. They had to tell the judge that I was abducted and forced to do all of these things against my will. They found me and they protected him. They removed me from all of that.

I found a folder named 'Blaine ' and I opened it.

There are documents pertaining to my court cases. There are pictures of me as a little kid with my dead birth parents that my parents never let me see. I see a thumbnail for the video of me killing my mom.

I opened the video.

I skip ahead to the part where the woman behind the camera tells me "Good boy Blaine, you did good." I replayed those words several times, I swear I know that voice.

I don't immediately notice that the video is a couple seconds longer and I let it continue playing. The woman walks over to me and hugs me. We both turn around and walk hand in hand back towards the camera. I pause the picture once the woman's face becomes clear.

It is Mother. Mother abducted me. She forced me to murder my birth mom. She is the one who has been behind this all along. Why? Why would she do this to me?

I close the video and I keep looking through the folder.

I found an icon for the instant messenger program. I click on it and the login information comes up. SoccerDude2k1 is the screen name.

"Are you fucking kidding me?" I question myself. "They were behind this too?"

There is one last video on the desktop labeled "Order of Azoth" . I click it and a sort of recruitment or propaganda video begins to play explaining their history and objectives.

The Order of Azoth as we know it today is rooted in world history and is the longest running form of continuous organized belief systems in the world. Our doctrine of beliefs predates Christianity, Judaism, Islam and every other current day religion.

The name Azoth is rooted in alchemy from approximately 100 BC. Prior to the name Order of Azoth we were simply referred to as "Incolae Primi" roughly meaning first people. Azoth was Believed to be the Universal Solvent, Universal Cure, and Elixir of Life. It is widely regarded as the embodiment of all other substances and the root of transformation essential to evolution and change.

The Order of Azoth has gained its acclaim and wealth throughout the years by investing and diversifying its members into all facets of society. From the dawn of the order we began as spice traders, fur traders, blacksmiths, alchemists and human traders. The latter being what really brought the Order into the power that it has seen today.

Human beings have always thirsted for power and control whether it be in the form of running countries, cities, plantations or just owning another human being. We specialized in the sales of humans to others for the purposes of work, sex and ritual sacrifices and as time has gone on and society has evolved we have noticed that this human desire has not faded at all. We now specialize in human trafficking with a specific focus on children, that is where we really make our quotas and meet monetary goals for the year.

That was enough for me, I shut the video off because I couldn't stomach another second. I knew where the video was heading from there. Child pornography, selling children into human sex trafficking and my parents were playing a large part in it, not only that they were grooming me as a child to become a part of it.

I open the door and walk downstairs to where my parents are sitting. I opened the fridge and I grabbed out three beers. I set a beer down in front of both of them at the table. I took a seat between my parents, I opened my beer and I took a drink of it. I looked at Father then I looked over at Mother.

They both stare back at me, waiting for me to speak. They can tell that I know now. They wanted me to know all along. They can finally have me back, I can finally fulfill my destiny.

"Just please tell me why? Why all of those children? Why Me?" I ask them.

Chapter Twenty

The waiter comes to the table and sets a large plate in the middle of the table. "We have three different types of crème brulee for you. Caramel, coffee and honey. I have also brought out for each of you a glass of French Moscato to pair with your dessert. Enjoy"

Megan finally breaks her silence "I am so sorry Blaine, I had no idea.

"You don't have to be sorry Megan, that's why I wanted to tell you all of this. I needed to you to know all of this about me."'

"That is horrible, Blaine. I am just speechless, I can't believe you had to go through all of that. What did your parents tell you? Why did they do it?"

"I'm getting to that," Blaine tells Megan.

"Blaine, my parents and your father's parents have been a part of this collection of people for a very long time. These are very powerful people, Blaine. People have become presidents and CEO's because of their family history being involved with the Order" Mother explains to me.

Father begins to explain to me "It is extremely common in the group for children to be arranged to marry each other, that is the case with your Mother and I. Our parents met with each other when we were children and they decided that we would spend our lives together" Father goes on.

"Maybe that's why the orgies and the group sex is so prevalent amongst all of us because we never really got an opportunity to explore that for ourselves. I battle internally with that all the time but I know at the end of the day I love your father and the life that we have created with each other is the life that I would choose to live even if it weren't with him" Mother passionately tries to explain herself to me.

"That's all fine and well but why did you abduct me? And what happened to my parents?" I asked them.

"Well, we weren't exactly lying then we told you that your parents were junkies Blaine. I'm sure by now you have done enough research to find out that your parents were actually cops. We kind of just stole that back story from them because we thought it would make a simple transition for you in your new home. But your parents were corrupt, they were dirty and they were drug addicts" Mother tells me.

"One day they sold you out to one of our members for sex when you were eight years old. He didn't have sex with you or plan to have sex with you, at least that is what he told us. Your parents never came back to get you. So we took you in and we fed you. Then your parents wanted to play the part of some loving parents whose son went missing and they were dying to find him. So we abducted your parents and naturally we killed your father, we burned his body because he was of no use to us. But your Mother on the other hand knew exactly what we wanted to do with her" Father tells me.

"Yeah, I saw the video," I told them.

"It was your rite of passage Blaine. The only way that you could truly get away from that life of constant abuse and neglect was to kill your birth mother. Your Father and I wanted a little boy but we were unable to have children of our own. You were heaven sent to us, you came to us in a time of need. We were starting to give up hope and our marriage was starting to fall apart and one day you just came into our lives. You were an amazing child and your piece of shit parents did not deserve you Blaine" Mother starts to cry as she is telling me all of this.

"I can see why you would do all of that for me but there are a lot of things that I am not okay with. The first being all of the child exploitation that goes on. It is absolutely disgusting the amount of pedophiles you would allow to be around your child" I explain to them.

"Blaine, that type of behavior has been going on since the beginning of time, it is nothing new. Civilizations have been buying and selling children as brides for thousands of years. We made sure that no one would ever touch you" Father tells me.

"It's not just about me, Father. There are hundreds if not thousands of little boys and girls out there whose lives were ruined because of us. I'm sure that is something that some people cannot recover from. Finding out that their body or pictures and videos of their bodies are being sold for some perverts sexual gratification" I am angrily starting to voice my disgust to them.

"That is such a small piece of what we do Blaine , I'm sure we would be able to cut all of that out. They want you Blaine, they know that you are special. They know what you are capable of and they have always looked to you to be the next one to lead all of us. You have something in you Blaine , something that makes you different. You weren't born into this, you chose to become a part of all of this, that makes you special" Mother sobbingly tells me.

"If I was to be a part of this I want to be completely done with anything involving sex trafficking or any of that other disgusting pedophile shit. I'm sure there are a million other ways we can make money" I explained to them.

"Absolutely buddy. Child pornography is just an easy buck in a niche market. Those chat rooms and message boards are always being investigated and shut down by the FBI , we're past due on doing away with all of that. Where we really make their money is in lobbying and politics. Not only that but also by laundering money through mega churches and in funding private prisons" Father explains to me. "There is a whole underground network of millions of people that are constantly funneling tax dollars and donations to aid in whatever it is that we decide we need to fund. There is an unlimited supply of manpower and resources. Government propaganda videos, music festivals, hell we even released fifteen movies in Hollywood last year" Father begins bragging to me.

"How can we get rid of these pedophiles? I want to kill them all. It might be a little much to ask immediately but that is what I want. If you want me to take you all seriously that is what I want. Anyone who has hurt children or violated a child in any way I want them gone. The community has no place for people like that, people with disgusting fetishes and a desire to pray on human beings who can't stand up for themselves. They all must die and we have to do it" I am now beginning to speak with a confidence that my parents have never seen come from me before.

"That is asking a lot Blaine. There are probably at least two hundred people in our area alone that would fit that description, let alone the thousands of others across the world" Father says.

"That's it? Two hundred people around here and thousands across the world? Can't you see that out of millions of people in this cult there are only a few thousand that get off on this type of deviant behavior? They need to be killed. They need to be killed as soon as possible, and we need to do as many as we can at once."

"You need to plan another one of your sacrificial orgy parties or whatever it is that you call them, but be extremely specific about who you invite. I'm sure there is a way that we would be able to take care of everyone in one quick act" I tell my parents hoping that they are on board.

My parents agreed to host another party and we all began planning it.

Megan chimes into the conversation.

"So you and your parents planned a party where you would get a bunch of pedophiles together and you would kill all of them?"

"Yeah pretty much. My parents were in charge, these people had no choice but to come."

"Well, why didn't you just tell the cops or something?"

"The cops wouldn't have done anything Megan. These people had gotten away with this kind of behavior for decades. It was up to me to put an end to it."

"Your plan was to put an end to it by pretending that you wanted to be the new leader of this pedophile sex cult and then murdering a bunch of people in front of your parents or with your parents ...and then what? Were you going to kill your parents too because they were part of that cult?"

"Just let me explain everything and you will get it Megan."

"You keep saying that to me Blaine but nothing seems to be getting any more clear or make any more sense. All of this is extremely out there stuff." Megan says to Blaine.

Blaine explains the details that his parents and him came together and executed.

We planned for everyone to come over to my parents house where we would have a girl there to stage a ritual sacrifice.

Megan cuts in again "Where did you get this girl?"

"My parents knew her, can I go on?"

"Yeah go on."

So we invited over around twenty people, men and women that were locally involved in creating and distributing child pornography. People that had been doing these disgusting horrible things for a very long time, people that needed to be stopped.

So when they got there and they saw the sacrifice was going on everyone usually partakes in drinking blood after they begin to start the bloodletting on the victim.

"So you actually killed this girl just to get back at all these pedophiles?" Megan asks.

"Yes. My parents knew her and they told me that she was willing to die for their cause."

"You mean die for your cause? Because now you were the leader of this cult."

"Will you please just let me finish? Everything will make sense."

So after the blood letting my parents collected a large jug of the blood and they spiked it with cyanide and ricin. The smell of blood and the consistency easily masked it so that no one would suspect a thing. After all of the people drank the blood like they normally do they all died. Then my parents and I took all of the bodies including the girls and we took them to the funeral home of one of the members and we cremated them all together.

"Blaine. You killed an innocent girl, then you collected her blood and you used it as a way to poison and kill all of them people. Then you took all of their bodies and you burned them? Do you not see how fucked up all of this is?" Megan hysterically explains to Blaine.

"No, I know that it's fucked up. But I'm trying to explain to you how I made it all better."

After we burned the bodies, I immediately went to the police. I reported myself and I reported my parents and I reported every single instance of crime and murder and rape and abduction that I could possibly find in all of the records that were kept. I alerted the FBI to the status of the cult and the names of everyone I could find.

My parents were arrested and they were charged, about 300 people were found and arrested and charged in connection to the cult.

I did everything I possibly could to make sure that no one else would get hurt going forward. I knew that I did horrible things and I wanted to fix that. So I turned myself in.

The FBI, the CIA, the state police, and everyone in law enforcement interviewed me. They determined that because

I was so messed up from being kidnapped then raised by my captors and hidden away for so long they didn't want to try me for any of the crimes. They were thankful and quite frankly extremely surprised that I was even able to be cognizant of the fact that everything they were doing was wrong and that I had the ability to turn them in.

So they put me into witness protection, they were able to help me find a new job, they moved me here and the rest is history.

Now I am sitting here in this amazing restaurant with the most beautiful woman on the planet. I have come to terms with my horrible past. I have decided that I will not let that control me.

The Order of Azoth is dead. Blaine Holly is dead. Blaine Acadia is dead. But I am alive.

Megan is speechless, they are at a standoff as Blaine racks his brain on his next move.

"How did you not remember coaxing all of those children into sending you pictures and participating in doing those things Blaine?" Megan asks.

"After I was taken away from my parents for a little while I guess they must have put me through some very extensive levels of counseling to make me forget that I participated in all of that."

"Do you think there is a chance that it was your parents that brainwashed you to make you forget your participation in everything? Then when you got older they decided it would be the right time to clue you back in?"

"I guess that would be possible, they don't really seem like the type of people who would know how to do something like that though."

"Are you blind Blaine? You just explained to me how your parents are the most well connected people in this country, maybe even in the world. Even if your parents don't know how to, I'm sure they would know someone who was capable of it. Maybe the FBI or whoever else you called was in on it too. Blaine, are you sure we are even safe just sitting here right now? Do you think there is a chance that we were followed? Have we been being followed the whole time that I've known you?"

"No Megan, all of that is behind me. No one knows where I am. We are safe, you are the only person who knows me now."

Chapter Twenty One

"Now that I have shared with you my whole fucked up life story I am hoping that you can accept my past and you can help me build my future."

Blaine gets down on one knee and grabs Megan's hand.

"Megan, will you make me the happiest man in the world by marrying me?"

Megan gets up from the table and she bursts out in tears. She runs to the front of the restaurant and into the women's bathroom.

Blaine stays sitting at the table. He has a million thoughts racing through his mind ranging from thoughts of self harm to anger towards Megan.

He shared with her something that he has never shared with anyone else before and her only reaction was to run away. Blaine sits alone in silence at the table for several minutes sipping at what is left of the bottles of wine.

Megan reappears from the front of the restaurant and she walks over to Blaine. She grabs him by the hands and she pulls him upward so that they are standing face to face.

"When I was fourteen years old, my parents had a bunch of friends over to their house for a party. I thought that it was just going to be a normal party, my parents hosted them all of the time. My parents and their friends were all in the backyard drinking and swimming in our pool so I decided I would just go upstairs to my room and lay in bed and watch a movie. Around ten o'clock at night my Mother and my father came into my room. They told me that because I was fourteen I was now a woman and that I was expected to start participating in activities that women participate in.

I wasn't sure what they meant by that, but they were going to fill me in whether or not I wanted to.

They led me by my hand downstairs where there were men and women waiting for me, naked. These men and women I had gone my whole life trusting, they watched me grow up from the time I was born until that day. They came to my soccer games, they babysat me, they taught me how to talk and how to walk, I trusted them.

Before I could really make sense of what was happening they were swarming me. They were kissing me, they were touching me, they were telling me how pretty I was. They were caressing me in places that I had never been touched, they were putting fingers in places I had never been touched, they were kissing me in places that only I was ever allowed to see.

On that day my parents forced me to become what they saw as a woman. It didn't just happen and end quickly, they guilted me into playing a part in their disgusting orgy for several hours.

Then when they were done and they ensured that I had all that I could handle they led me into the backyard. They walked me out to a fire where there were two people covered in some kind of cloak. A woman pulled a dagger out from her cloak and she summoned me over to her. My parents dragged me to the lady and she inserted the dagger into me, she put it right inside of me, in the place where no one had been prior to that night.

The man in the other cloak pulled out a chalice and he began collecting the blood that was flowing out from inside of me. He held it there for several minutes until the chalice was full of my blood, once it was full everyone gathered in a circle around me and the fire.

They began to chant as they all took turns drinking from the cup that contained the fresh blood that was forced out of me from my once pure and innocent young girl's body.

I must have blacked out because I don't remember anything beyond that. I woke up the next morning in my bed, clothed and my parents were downstairs eating breakfast like nothing had happened."

Blaine is trying to find the words to comfort Megan at that moment, he knows who her parents are now. That can't be a coincidence.

"I ran away from home that day and I never looked back at Blaine."

"I just can't believe…"

Megan cuts him off mid sentence.

"Yes, absolutely I will, I will marry you Blaine."

Blaine leans in to kiss Megan.

"Wait, wait I want to take a picture of our first kiss as an engaged couple" she says as she reaches into her purse and pulls out her phone to take a picture.

Blaine looks around and everyone in the restaurant has begun to pile into the back area where he and Megan were sitting. He smiles and thanks everyone as they are clapping and staring at the huge display of romanticism.

"Well at least I got the proposal right" Blaine tells Megan as he leans in and kisses her on the lips.

Megan takes a picture of them.

"I will cherish the picture for the rest of my life."

The waiter comes to the table and pours them both a glass of champagne.

"Congratulations to you both" he says as he pours the champagne. "Cheers to you both and I wish you both the best."

The waiter walks away from the table to the kitchen area.

Blaine and Megan raise their glasses and they tap them together.

"To us," Blaine says.

Megan nods "To us."

Blaine puts the champagne flute to his lips and drinks the whole glass.

"Cheers sweetheart, drink up" Megan says as Blaine is drinking.

Blaine looks at Megan who is just staring at him as if she's waiting for something to happen.

Blaine begins to feel his throat closing up.

"You can't stop us Blaine, you were stupid to think you ever could" Megan says as Blaine grips his throat.

He starts gurgling and fighting to catch his breath as he stands up from the table.

Blaine falls face first onto the floor and foam starts to pour from Blaine's mouth. The blood vessels begin to burst in his eyes and face and he starts to turn from pale white to blue and red.

Megan walks over to Blaine and kneels down next to him. This is going to sound very familiar Blaine, you showed these words to me, I might paraphrase just a little bit but tell me if I'm on the right track.

"Boy, we gave you every opportunity."

She kisses him on the cheek.

"We gave you our hands to get you off your knees."

She puts her ear to his mouth and nose to see if he is still breathing.

"You sat at our table and you ate everything."

217

She slides her fingers down his eyelids to close his eyes.

"You say that you're still hungry, then bite the plates and break your teeth."

She kisses him one last time on the lips.

Everyone in the restaurant begins to gather around them and begin clapping at the sight of Blaine's death. Megan stands to her feet. She is standing not just for herself but she is standing on behalf of countless others.

Though Megan stands just above five feet tall at that moment she towers over Blaine's limp body. Her mere presence and obvious glaring levels of eminence had cast a long shadow for Blaine to bask in since the day they first met.

"He's suffered enough already, give him the shot" Megan hears a voice say as she looks back to see the familiar voice coming from the crowd and she sees Mother emerge from the sea of faces surrounding her.

Megan nods and she reaches into her purse.

She pulls out a hypodermic needle attached to a syringe and she drives it into Blaine's chest cavity as she pushes down on the plunger.

Blaine almost instantly jolts back to consciousness, his vision is blurry and his memory is foggy but he slowly is starting to piece together where he is and the events that had just unfolded.

He looks up at Megan standing over him and his vision pans to her side and he sees his Mother standing next to her.

"You are supposed to be in prison. I watched them take you away" Blaine tells Mother .

Mother speaks up again "take him to the sanctuary."

A group of men emerge from the crowd and they grab Blaine, they cover his head with a black cloth bag. They grab Blaine's arms and they tie his arms behind his back. Blaine is still in a fog and not completely sure if what is going on is a dream or reality. He feels men begin to grab his legs and he starts to struggle as best as he can. He pulls and pushes and kicks but he is too weak to really put up any kind of true fight. His legs are tied together and he is carried out of the restaurant and thrown head first into a van waiting for them out front.

Blaine is laying on his back and starts to feel a warm liquid running from the top of his head down his face and the mask starts to fill. The liquid inches up past his chin and Blaine recognizes the taste, it is blood. It moves up past his mouth and he begins breathing through his nose until the blood fills past his nose. The bag is filling up faster and faster until it is covering his eyes. He is able to move his head around enough to find an air pocket small enough for him to continue breathing. He starts to feel dizzy and he's unsure if it's the drugs kicking in again or from the loss of blood.

The van takes off down the street and three police cars lead the way. Mother and Megan get into an SUV trailing behind the van providing an escort to ensure they get Blaine to the sanctuary uninterrupted. They are sitting in silence for several minutes before Mother begins to speak.

"I am very proud of you Megan. You have done everything that has ever been asked of you and your time of true power and glory is soon approaching."

Megan is staring at Mother and Mother grabs her hand and begins to caress Megan's cheek with the back of her hand. Megan closes her eyes and she begins to have a flashback to the first time she and Mother met.

Megan is sitting in her bedroom and she hears footsteps coming up the stairs headed toward her. The door opens and a woman walks into her room. Megan's parents are standing behind the woman in the doorway as if they are preventing her from running out..

"Do you remember me, Megan? From when you were little?" the woman asks.

Megan looks at her closely, she looks her up and down and examines every detail of her face.

"I don't think I do maam" Megan replies to the woman.

"That really is a shame. How about from the ceremony Megan? I was the conductor. They call me the Harbinger, but you can just refer to me as Mother" the woman tells Megan.

"I think I might remember you now, that all sounds familiar."

"We have very big plans for you Megan. I know you are only sixteen now but you have been chosen. I have a son Megan, his name is Blaine. He is nearly twenty years old. In a few years he is going to be ready to marry and have children and become the new Harbinger and we want you for his wife. You don't have to acknowledge me or my offer and agree to this now but it is something you need to think about, and you absolutely cannot tell anyone else. If anyone inside or outside of the Order of Azoth were to find out it would create exceptional levels of jealousy and dissension toward our regime and what we are trying to create."

Megan sits in silence. Mother stands up and she gives Megan a kiss on the cheek.

"I look forward to meeting with you again in a few years Megan." Mother walks out of the room.

Megan opens her eyes and she and Mother are still sitting in the back of the SUV and Mother grabs Megan's hand. "I chose you for a reason Megan. You are strong. You are kind. You are smart. You are beautiful. You are everything that the Order of Azoth needs in a Harbinger."

This conversation causes Megan's brain to rapidly begin to replay hundreds of past memories of her and Mother but one especially stands out to her, this one not too far in the past.

Megan and Mother are sitting together at a coffee table in Megan's childhood home.

"Blaine is going to turn on us Megan. We have people in place to take him away and place him into protective custody. Once he is placed we need you to move with him. You will organically run into him at a coffee shop or something and ask him out. He will instantly fall in love with you. When you begin to think that he plans to ask you to be his wife we will go from there. We need you to constantly check in with us and keep us filled in on details. You must completely appeal to him in every way. It is essential to the Order of Azoth that both prospective Harbingers come together and our time to complete this all is starting to get extremely thin Megan."

Mother and Megan hear a loud screeching and grinding and the SUV slams to a sudden stop.

"Why the hell have we stopped?" Mother asks the driver.

"The van in front of us slammed on its brakes" the driver of the SUV looks back and explains.

Mother scans the road up ahead of her. She sees a railroad crossing has been activated and the only vehicle in front of them is the van that Blaine is in stopped about five feet away and all she can make out is the back of the van with no ground in between.

"The police cars in front must have gone through the crossing before it activated and the van stopped for some reason" the driver tells Mother .

"Well then get out and see what the hell is going on" Mother shouts at the driver.

Mother sees the driver get out of the car and he starts to walk toward the back of the van and suddenly he disappears.

Blaine pulls the driver to the ground between the two vehicles and he begins to choke the driver until he passes out.

Blains gets into the front seat of the SUV where Mother and Megan are sitting in the back and they take off.

"Mother, I see you and Megan have already gotten to know each other, but something tells me this isn't the first time that you two have gotten to meet and if things go my way now you will get to spend eternity together in hell."

Blaine stomps on the gas and drives through the railroad crossing arm and slams on the brakes to stop on the tracks. He presses the lock buttons on the doors to ensure that neither Mother or Megan can escape. He slowly turns the SUV toward the train and he looks back at Mother and

Megan. Megan has begun to cry and frantically pulls at the door handles as she is begging for Blaine to let her out.

Blaine floors the gas pedal again and races down the train tracks to meet the train head on. He looks back at Mother and Megan one more time before the lights from the train blind everyone inside of the SUV.

The train is blowing its horn and the sound is getting louder and louder until it's too late for any of them to get out of the way.

The train horn is blowing, Blaine can see the conductor motioning for them to get out of the way until the man disappears into the blinding lights of the train and all he can see is an out of focus blue force he can only assume to be the front end of the unrelenting pissed off locomotive.

The 150 ton steel locomotive cuts through the SUV with ease as it travels well over 100 MPH and everyone inside of the SUV is torn to pieces and any identifying characteristics of living and breathing human beings practically evaporates into thin air from the impact.

Chapter Twenty Two

Blaine is jarred back into consciousness as his fabricated act of revenge and destruction is enough to awake from his temporary coma and he comes to feeling disheveled, distraught and physically sickened with an overwhelming sense of betrayal.

He begins to roll around to feel his surroundings and he is still in the back of the van and is not sure if his consciousness is a figmented version of reality from the drugs or an actual living nightmare as he feels aching all over from the beating he took shortly before being stuffed in the back of the van.

The door opens and Blaine sees a slight outline of a hand reaching toward him as the cover is pulled from his eyes. He sees Megan and Mother standing outside of the van looking intently at him.

"Megan, you knew about this all along, didn't you?" Blaine asks Megan.

"I did Blaine."

"Why would you go along with this?" Blaine asks.

"She will not be made to feel ashamed for doing what she was born to do, Blaine. You and her were meant to rule together and you turned your back on that. You will not try to make her feel guilty, you are the one who should feel guilty for letting thousands of us down." Mother says to

Blaine. She turns to two men who are standing nearby awaiting their arrival "take him inside and put him in the Harbinger suite."

Megan looks at Mother standing next to her "you are letting him stay in the Harbinger suite?"

"Not just him Megan, both of you. We still have to go forward with this sacrifice, the future of this depends on it. He may not want to rule but someone still has to Megan, you know what you have to do." Mother says to Megan.

"I understand Mother."

Blaine is taken into the house and walked down a long hallway dimly lit with pictures of prior Harbingers lining the walls. The floor is a hardwood covered mostly in a red runner that ends at a large white French door at the end. The men open the door and Blaine is carried into a bedroom. His hands and feet are untied and he is thrown onto a bed.

"Don't move until we leave this room or you'll get beaten even worse than the first time" one of the men says as they walk out of the room.

Blaine hears the door lock from the outside and he runs to the door and tries to open it. He punches and kicks the door and throws his shoulder into it several times but the door doesn't move an inch. Blaine is locked in the room.

Blaine begins pacing back and forth in front of the bed planning a way to possibly escape from the room. The room is very large with dark gray walls and white wainscoting around the entire area. There are several windows but as Blaine tries to open them he sees men standing outside of each of them guarding from his escape. He opens a door that leads into a large bathroom area with a big jetted marble bathtub, the floor is marble, the shower is marble and the vanity is marble, Blaine looks up and there is a large skylight window at the top of the vaulted ceiling about 15 feet up. Blaine scans the bathroom for a chair to stand on but quickly realizes it is too high. Blaine walks back out of the bathroom and sits on the bed and tries to think of another way to escape for several minutes until he hears footsteps approaching the door. He looks around the room and picks up a chair sitting in front of a nearby night stand and prepares to use it as a weapon.

Blaine hears a lock open and the door handle turns and the door opens, Megan walks through the door and stands in the doorway. "Oh would you please put that chair down Blaine, we both know that you don't have it in you" Megan enters the room to talk with Blaine.

Megan walks over near Blaine and she sits on the end of the bed. She pats the bed next to her to motion for Blaine to sit down next to her. He begrudgingly does so.

"Look around you Blaine, this bedroom is gorgeous and it could be ours. This bedroom is just the beginning of what would be ours too Blaine. This is just one small room in one small home in one small city in a world that we own. We have to do this Blaine. This is our destiny. Yes all of this was planned and yes I did trick you but I love you

Blaine and we owe it to ourselves to take what is rightfully ours.."

Blaine sits in silence.

"All of this is going to go forward whether or not you agree to it. If you agree to it then you and I can share the power, we can both make decisions together. We can rule with love and compassion and we can make changes for the better, we can do that together. But if you don't agree then you will force me to turn everyone against you once we assume power, which won't be hard to do. They might kill you or they might just take you away forever and torture you, I'm not sure to the extent of what this crime would call for."

"Megan, why do you want this so badly? I told you what these people do. I told you who they are, why would you want to be a part of that?" Blaine asks Megan.

"They molested me Blaine. They inserted a blade inside of me and they cut me. They cut me open and they tasted me, but that's not just it Blaine, they stole every bit of innocence from me that they could and I want to get back at them. I want them to suffer for doing that to me. I know it was not only me that they hurt Blaine. I have to kill Mother and Father for what they did to me as a child. I knew this was the only way to get revenge for it. By assuming the role of the new Harbingers we get to kill the old."

"So your plan is to get back at them by joining their cult?"

"Get back at them by killing them by taking from them the only thing that they ever really cared about. Then after I kill them or we kill them we can kill everyone else that is not worthy of this great blessing."

Blaine is now realizing Megan's plan.

"Once we are in charge we can kill everyone involved in the order? Is that what you think will happen? They have been around for a very long time Megan, people are not just going to listen to us right away. Even if they do eventually listen to us do you actually think they will just let us start killing all of their members? This is their parents, their siblings, their spouses and their children were talking about."

"I promise you they will Blaine. These members are loyal to the Order and to the Harbingers and that is it. Once your parents surrender their power to us the members will have no choice but to follow our new directives. Every time a new Harbinger comes into power they sculpt the Order to the image that they believe best for all of its members and if that image means that some people have to die then they will die. Whether they choose to take their own lives or they are forced into the fire, they will die."

"But do we really want to take over this cult, Megan?"

"We will be two of the most powerful people in America. We will have to overhaul what this all stands for. We can kill all of the people who have harmed children, kill everyone who uses violence against children to make money. We can really do good Blaine. We will be in charge and no one can question us."

Blaine agrees with Megan "It is sickening they have sunk this low. We have our hands in politics, in banking, in sports and nearly everything else in this country but my parents have let pedophilia go on this long for what?"

Megan kisses Blaine on the lips and stands up "now you are starting to see, I'll be back shortly my love."

Megan leaves the room, she goes through the house and outside where Mother is waiting for her.

"He has agreed to wed me Mother, he has agreed to take over."

"He knows he must kill his father and I in order for you both to become the new harbingers?"

"I think that is the only reason he agreed to do it, Mother."

"After all of this time you still don't see the plan here do you Megan?"

"The plan to put Blaine in charge?"

"Don't be so naive Megan. He loves you, he will do anything for you but you are the one we want to lead, you always have been. Blaine is just a pawn. Megan when we abducted Blaine it was because we knew a male needed to be the figurehead for all of this, but it has always been the women harbingers that have been in charge. Did your parents ever tell you how they came about raising you?"

"No? What do you mean?"

"Megan. You are our first birth child. Sadly because you were born a female we could not leave the fate of the order in your hands. We gave you away to your parents to raise you with the agreement that when you were of age we would find a male for you to be with. That is why we took Blaine. We took Blaine and we raised him to be a perfect submissive spouse for you. Someone who would never challenge your lead. We love you Megan and everything we have done has been to ensure you will truly lead as the true Harbinger of the Order of Azoth."

"If you were the true Harbinger yourself why didn't you just change the rules so that a female could lead?" Megan asks Mother.

"It's not that simple Megan. There are rules that are in place and have been in place for a very long time. Times are changing but certain things are expected of the women that stand aside the men in place."

"You gave me away because you were too afraid to challenge these men and their outdated chauvinistic views? Then you kidnapped some innocent boy and you brainwashed him? All so you could hope to make it up to me in the future? You are truly crazy, do you know that?"

"It is not that simple Megan. I love you, and you deserve to take your rightful place. That is why I did this. Maybe by the time your reign comes to an end you can change some things but I could not and I did what I could to ensure that you would be here today. Now go get ready, the ceremony is about to start. Go and take your rightful place as the true Harbinger."

Two men in red cloaks enter Blaine's room and they grab him. Blaine is blindfolded and led outside by the men. The men walk him outside with Blaine and remove the blindfold.

Blaine is standing before a collection of men and women in cloaks, half of them are red and half of them are black. Mother and Father are standing at the pulpit in red cloaks with Megan in black and everyone is staring at Blaine waiting for him to approach.

Mother motions for the men to bring Blaine to them.

"There will be a sacrifice tonight. A man and a woman must die in order for the new Harbingers to assume total control. As the custom has always stated, in order for the new regime to have total power and control the old regime must perish in flame. That is why we are here tonight. Our son Blaine after all these years and through numerous obstacles has finally decided to acknowledge his place as the heir to the Order of Azoth. Alongside his soon to be beautiful wife Megan they will be the new Harbingers."

Father steps forward "My son, take your wife hand in hand."

Megan takes his right hand and Blaine grabs Megan's hand across from him.

Father pulls a dagger from his cloak and he slices open Blaine's left palm. He reaches to Megan and grabs her right hand and he slices open her right palm.

Megan recognizes the dagger from the ceremony that stole her innocence.

Father grabs their hands and places them together. Both of their hands dripping in blood "You are both now forever bound to each other. If one of you were to die, you both are to die. If one of you were to leave the other you both must parish, this oath is for life."

Mother grabs Father by his hands and they look into each other's eyes. "You know what we must do now" Mother says to Father.

Father hands the dagger to Megan. "Our new Harbinger, a female, must take the life of the old female." Mother looks at Megan and nods to her, she lifts Megan's hand and she guides her hand with the dagger into her chest. Mother removes the dagger and she hands it to Blaine.

Blaine takes the dagger and he drives it into Father's chest. Mother and Father embrace as they walk towards the open fire that is roaring in front of the assembly of people.

"We must perish together and like our love has burned for decades, as tradition now states and since the dawn of time has stated, we must now burn as well" Mother says as she and Father parade into the open fire pit.

"Gather everyone together now and start a broadcast to all members" Megan exclaims.

All of the members take out their phones and begin to record and broadcast live to the other members of the order that are not in attendance.

"Blaine and I stand before you here today as your new Harbingers. We are now the faces of the future and the hands you must turn to and depend on for leadership and guidance. They say that a new broom sweeps clean and we are that new broom. We look to completely repair and reconstruct this broken system that thrives on abuse, exploitation and fear" Megan says to the assembly.

"As the children of the former Harbingers we were mistreated. We were sexually and physically abused. We were abducted, we were discarded, we were exploited and when we challenged these decisions we were forsaken and they attempted to reprogram us like we were machines. But here we stand now, together, ready to lead, serve and command all of you" Blaine exclaims to the assembly.

"All that we ask of you is one thing going forward to start, we need you to listen to us and this directive very clearly. This is not going to be open for debate or discussion, this is not a suggestion, this is not an idea, this is not a recommendation. This is a clear and concise order and a failure to follow this order will result in immediate termination." Megan says directly to the red and black cloaks in attendance.

Megan and Blaine look at each other, they grab one another's hand and they look to the crowds of cameras and speak in unison.

"If you or someone you know has ever sexually abused a child whether it be physically or mentally in any way it is imperative to the Order of Azoth that they must be punished, by means no lesser than execution or if you have any dignity we will allow it by self sacrifice. We must eradicate these people and this behavior from within our ranks, there will be no exceptions and any attempt to avoid compliance with this order as we previously stated will result in the execution of all parties involved for treason."

Everyone in attendance begins chanting "for the new Harbingers" and "for the order". They draw daggers from their cloaks and members wearing red cloaks are all pushed to the front.

"Who are these members in the red cloaks?" Blaine asks Megan.

"Those in red cloaks were identified prior to the ritual by Mother and Father as sacrifices as a parting gift to us Blaine. In order for a new regime to take place all members must subscribe to the new Harbingers belief system. Any possible dissenters and anyone who contributed to pedophilia in any form were identified by their red cloaks and told they would be chosen as advisors to gain their compliance." Megan explains to Blaine.

"So all of these people are willingly going to die?" Blaine asks Megan.

"Well, they are going to die, whether it be willingly or forcefully, everyone here knows that the order comes before ego and before self. If they don't willingly accept their punishment they will die with embarrassment and shame."

"You step forward," Megan points to a young woman in the crowd.

"I want you to be the sole documentation of this, keep your camera going and make sure you get everything. Everyone else put your cameras away."

Nearly all of the live cameras immediately begin to go black as phones are turned off or put away.

Megan points to the camera and the camera pans to the fire to show the scene of the bodies of the disgraced pedophiles and abusers being burned alive.

The screams from those in the red cloaks can be heard as hundreds of disgraced members of the Order of Azoth in attendance are forced into the fire all at once. The red cloaks are given the option to march into the fire on their own and die with dignity and the promise of a place in the afterlife or be killed and burned with disgrace and marked as betrayers and be banished to an eternity of emptiness.

The camera turns back to Megan and Blaine.

Megan grabs Blaine's hand and they position themselves ready to deliver parting words to everyone in attendance and everyone watching the stream.

"Thank you for your support" Megan and Blaine say in unison to the camera as the broadcast feed closes.

Find Dissociation: A Collection of Short Stories on Amazon.

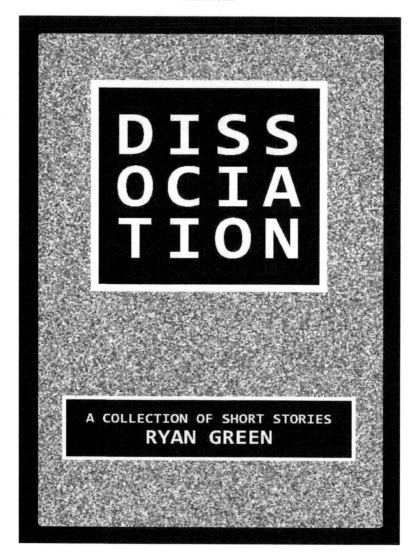

Made in the USA
Middletown, DE
11 September 2021

48077902R00136